'Extraordinary masterpieces of the twentieth century'
– John Banville

'A brilliant writer' – India Knight

'Intense atmosphere and resonant detail . . . make Simenon's fiction remarkably like life' – Julian Barnes

'A truly wonderful writer . . . marvellously readable – lucid, simple, absolutely in tune with the world he creates'
– Muriel Spark

'Few writers have ever conveyed with such a sure touch, the bleakness of human life' – A. N. Wilson

'Compelling, remorseless, brilliant' – John Gray

'A writer of genius, one whose simplicity of language creates indelible images that the florid stylists of our own day can only dream of' – *Daily Mail*

'The mysteries of the human personality are revealed in all their disconcerting complexity' – Anita Brookner

'One of the greatest writers of our time' – *The Sunday Times*

'I love reading Simenon. He makes me think of Chekhov'
– William Faulkner

'One of the great psychological novelists of this century'
– *Independent*

'The greatest of all, the most genuine novelist we have had in literature' – André Gide

'Simenon ought to be spoken of in the same breath as Camus, Beckett and Kafka' – *Independent on Sunday*

Georges Simenon was born on 12 February 1903 in Liège, Belgium, and died in 1989 in Lausanne, Switzerland, where he had lived for the latter part of his life. Between 1931 and 1972 he published seventy-five novels and twenty-eight short stories featuring Inspector Maigret.

Simenon always resisted identifying himself with his famous literary character, but acknowledged that they shared an important characteristic:

> My motto, to the extent that I have one, has been noted often enough, and I've always conformed to it. It's the one I've given to old Maigret, who resembles me in certain points . . . 'understand and judge not'.

Penguin is publishing the entire series of Maigret novels.

GEORGES SIMENON

Maigret and the Headless Corpse

Translated by HOWARD CURTIS

PENGUIN BOOKS

PENGUIN CLASSICS

UK | USA | Canada | Ireland | Australia
India | New Zealand | South Africa

Penguin Books is part of the Penguin Random House group of companies
whose addresses can be found at global.penguinrandomhouse.com.

First published in French as *Maigret et le corps sans tête* by Presses de la Cité 1955
This translation first published 2017
008

Copyright © Georges Simenon Limited, 1955
Translation copyright © Howard Curtis, 2017
GEORGES SIMENON ® Simenon.tm
MAIGRET ® Georges Simenon Limited
All rights reserved

The moral rights of the author and translator have been asserted

Set in 12.5/15 pt Dante MT Std
Typeset by Jouve (UK), Milton Keynes
Printed and bound in Great Britain by Clays Ltd, Elcograf S.p.A.

ISBN: 978–0–241–29726–1

Contents

1. The Naud Brothers' Discovery

The sky was just starting to lighten when Jules, the elder of the two Naud brothers, appeared on the deck of the barge, first his head, then his shoulders, then his big lanky body. Rubbing his as yet uncombed flax-coloured hair, he looked at the lock, Quai de Jemmapes on the left, Quai de Valmy on the right. A few minutes went by, time enough to roll a cigarette and smoke it in the coolness of the early morning, before a light came on in the little bar on the corner of Rue des Récollets.

Because of the dim light, the front of the bar was a harsher yellow than usual. Popaul, the owner, collarless and also uncombed, came out on to the pavement to remove the shutters.

Naud walked across the gangway and the quayside, rolling his second cigarette. When his brother Robert, almost as tall and raw-boned as he was, emerged in his turn from a hatch, he was able to see Jules leaning on the counter in the lighted bar and the owner pouring a shot of brandy into his coffee.

Robert seemed to be waiting his turn. He rolled a cigarette in the same way as his brother. When Jules came out of the bar, Robert, the younger of the two, walked off the barge, and they met in the middle of the street.

'I'm starting the engine,' Jules announced.

There were days when they didn't exchange more than ten sentences like that. Their boat was called the *Deux Frères* – the Two Brothers. They had married twin sisters, and both families lived on board.

Robert took the place of his elder brother in Popaul's bar, which smelled of coffee laced with brandy.

'Nice day,' said Popaul, who was short and fat.

Robert Naud merely looked through the window at the pink-tinged sky. The chimney pots on the roofs were the first thing in the landscape to take on life and colour. On the slates and tiles, and on some of the cobbles on the quayside, the cold of the last hours of night had left a thin layer of frost that was starting to fade.

The diesel engine could be heard spluttering. Puffs of black smoke emerged from the stern of the barge. Robert put some coins on the zinc counter, touched his cap with his fingertips and walked back across the quayside. The lock-keeper had appeared, in his uniform, and was getting the lock ready. There was the sound of footsteps in the distance, on Quai de Valmy, although nobody was yet visible. Children's voices came from the interior of the boat, where the women were making coffee.

Jules reappeared on deck, went to the stern, leaned over and frowned. His brother guessed what was wrong. They had loaded some freestone at Beauval, at Post 48 along the Canal de l'Ourcq. As almost always happened, they had taken on a few tonnes too many, and already the previous day, leaving the basin of La Villette and moving into the Canal Saint-Martin, they had stirred the sludge at the bottom.

There is usually no lack of water in March. But this year, it hadn't rained for two months, and they had to be sparing with the canal water.

The lock gates opened. Jules took up his position at the wheel. His brother went back on to the quayside to cast off. The propeller started turning and, as both of them had feared, it stirred up thick mud that rose to the surface, making big bubbles.

Leaning with his whole weight on the pole, Robert tried hard to move the bow of the boat away from the quayside. The propeller seemed to be turning without any progress being made. Accustomed to such things, the lock-keeper waited patiently, beating his hands together to warm himself.

There was a thump, then a worrying noise of clashing gears. Robert Naud turned to his brother, who stalled the engine.

Neither of them knew what was happening. The propeller hadn't touched the bottom, protected as it was by part of the rudder. Something must have got stuck in it, perhaps an old cable, such as were often found lying at the bottom of canals. If it was that, they would find it hard to shake off.

Still holding his pole, Robert headed for the stern, leaned over and tried to reach the propeller through the opaque water, while Jules went looking for a smaller pole and Laurence, his wife, put her head out through the hatch.

'What is it?'

'Don't know.'

In silence, they began to manoeuvre the two poles around the stalled propeller. After a few minutes, the lock-keeper, Dambois, whom everybody called Charles, came and stood on the quayside to watch them. He didn't ask any questions, merely puffed silently at his pipe, the stem of which had been mended with wire.

A few passers-by could be seen hurrying towards the République, as well as nurses in uniform heading for the Hôpital Saint-Louis.

'Have you got it?'

'I think so.'

'Is it a cable?'

'I have no idea.'

Jules Naud had hooked something. After a while, the object yielded, and more bubbles rose to the surface.

Slowly, he pulled out the pole, and as the hook broke the surface, a strange package appeared, wrapped in newspaper that had burst open.

It was a human arm, intact from the shoulder to the hand. In the water, it had taken on a pallid colour and the texture of a dead fish.

Depoil, the sergeant from the third district police station at the end of Quai de Jemmapes, was just finishing his night shift when the tall figure of the elder Naud brother appeared in the doorway.

'I'm just above the Récollets lock with our boat, the *Deux Frères*. The propeller stalled when we cast off and we dredged up a man's arm.'

Depoil, who had worked in the tenth arrondissement

for fifteen years, had the reaction that all the police officers informed of the case would have.

'A man's?' he echoed, incredulously.

'A man's, yes. The hand is covered in brown hair and . . .'

Periodically, a corpse was fished out of the Canal Saint-Martin, almost always because of the movement of a boat's propeller. Most often, the corpse was intact, and it would usually turn out to be a man, an old tramp, for example, who had drunk too much and slipped into the canal, or a criminal stabbed to death by a rival gang.

Dismembered bodies weren't rare, two or three a year on average, but invariably, as far back as Sergeant Depoil could remember, they were women. You immediately knew where to look. Nine times out of ten, if not more, it was a low-class prostitute, one of those you see prowling at night around patches of waste ground.

'A sex crime,' the report would conclude.

The police knew the local crowd and had up-to-date lists of all the criminals and dubious individuals. A few days generally sufficed to arrest the perpetrator of an ordinary offence, whether it was a theft from a market stall or an armed robbery. But it was rare for them to get their hands on one of these killers.

'Have you brought it with you?' Depoil asked.

'The arm?'

'Where did you leave it?'

'On the quayside. Is it all right for us to go? We have to get down to Quai de l'Arsenal. They're waiting for us to unload.'

The sergeant lit a cigarette, began by informing the

police emergency switchboard of the incident, then asked for the number of the local detective chief inspector, Monsieur Magrin.

'Sorry to wake you. Some barge people have just fished a human arm out of the canal ... No, a man's arm! ... That's what I thought, too ... What? ... He's here, yes ... I'll ask him ...'

He turned to Naud, without letting go of the receiver.

'Does it look as if it's been in the water for a long time?'

The elder Naud scratched his head.

'That depends what you call a long time.'

'Is it very decomposed?'

'Hard to say. In my opinion, it could have been there about two or three days ...'

The sergeant repeated this into the telephone.

'Two or three days ...'

Then, playing with his pencil, he listened to the inspector's instructions.

'Can we go through the lock?' Naud asked again when he had hung up.

'Not yet. As the inspector just said, it's quite possible that other pieces have got stuck to the barge, and if we let it go ahead we might lose them.'

'But I can't stay there for ever! There are already four boats behind us.'

The sergeant, who had asked for another number, was waiting for the reply.

'Hello? Victor? Did I wake you? You're already having your breakfast? Good. I have a job for you.'

Victor Cadet lived not far from there, in Rue du

Chemin-Vert, and a month rarely passed without his services being called for on the Canal Saint-Martin. Without any doubt, he was the man who had fished the largest number of ill-assorted objects, including human bodies, from the Seine and the canals of Paris.

'Just give me time to inform my assistant.'

It was seven o'clock in the morning. On Boulevard Richard-Lenoir, Madame Maigret, already washed and dressed and smelling of soap, was busy in her kitchen, making breakfast, while her husband was still asleep. At police headquarters on Quai des Orfèvres, Lucas and Janvier had come on duty at six, and it was Lucas who took the call about the discovery made in the canal.

'Strange!' he grunted to Janvier. 'They just fished an arm out of the Canal Saint-Martin, and it isn't a woman's.'

'Is it a man's?'

'What else could it be?'

'Could be a child's.'

That had happened, too, just once, three years earlier.

'Are you going to let the chief know?'

Lucas looked at the time, hesitated and shook his head. 'There's no rush. Let him at least have his coffee.'

By 7.50, a fairly large crowd had formed near the *Deux Frères*, and a policeman was keeping the onlookers at a distance from an object that lay on the flagstones, covered with a piece of tarpaulin. Victor Cadet's boat, which had been moored upstream, had been let through the lock and now came alongside the quay.

Cadet was a giant of a man. He looked as if he had had

his diving suit made to measure. His assistant, on the other hand, was a little old man who chewed tobacco as he worked and sent long jets of brown saliva into the water.

It was he who secured the ladder, primed the pump and finally screwed the huge brass sphere on to Victor's neck.

Two women and five children, all with hair so blond it was almost white, were standing in the stern of the *Deux Frères*; one of the women was pregnant, the other held a baby on her arm.

The sunlight was beating down on the buildings along Quai de Valmy, sunlight so bright and gay that it made you wonder why that stretch of the canal had such a sinister reputation. True, the paintwork on the fronts of the buildings was faded, the whites and yellows pale and washed out, but on this March morning, everything seemed as bright and clear as a painting by Utrillo.

Four barges were waiting behind the *Deux Frères*, with washing drying on lines and children being forced to keep quiet. The smell of tar dominated the less pleasant smell of the canal.

At 8.15, Maigret, who was finishing his second cup of coffee and wiping his mouth before smoking his first pipe, took the call from Lucas.

'A man's arm, you say?'

He, too, was surprised.

'Was anything else found?'

'Victor the diver is already at work. We have to clear the lock as soon as possible to avoid a bottleneck.'

'Who's been dealing with this so far?'

'Judel.'

He was an inspector from the tenth arrondissement, a dull but conscientious young man who could be relied on in the early stages of an investigation.

'Are you going over there, chief?'

'It's not a big detour.'

'Do you want one of us to join you there?'

'Who's in the office?'

'Janvier, Lemaire . . . Wait. Lapointe has just come in.'

Maigret hesitated for a moment. Here, too, it was sunny, and they had been able to half open the window. The case might be trivial and straightforward. If it was, Judel could continue to handle it. It's hard to know at the beginning! If the arm had been a woman's, Maigret wouldn't have hesitated to wager that the rest would be routine.

But because it was a man's arm, anything was possible. And if the case turned out to be a complicated one, if Maigret decided to take charge of the investigation, what happened in the next few days would depend partly on the choice he was about to make, because he preferred to continue and finish an investigation with the inspector who had begun it with him.

'Send Lapointe.'

It was a while since he had last worked closely with Lapointe, whose youth entertained him, as did his enthusiasm – and his embarrassment when he thought he had committed a blunder.

'Shall I inform the commissioner?'

'Yes. I'll probably be late for the briefing.'

It was 23 March. Spring had officially begun two days

earlier, and you could already feel it in the air, which couldn't be said every year. It was so warm that Maigret almost went out without a coat.

Out on Boulevard Richard-Lenoir, he hailed a taxi. There was no direct bus route, and this wasn't the kind of weather for shutting yourself up in the Métro. As he expected, he got to the Récollets lock before Lapointe. He found Inspector Judel leaning over the dark water of the canal.

'Anything else been found?'

'Not yet, chief. Victor's busy going all around the barge to make sure nothing's stuck to it.'

Ten more minutes went by. Lapointe was just emerging from one of the Police Judiciaire's little black cars when clear bubbles announced that Victor was about to break surface.

His assistant hastened to unscrew the brass helmet. Immediately, Victor lit a cigarette, looked around, recognized Maigret and gave him a friendly wave.

'Anything else?'

'Not in this area.'

'Can the barge go on its way?'

'I'm pretty certain it won't hit anything, apart from the sludge at the bottom.'

Robert Naud, who had heard this, yelled to his brother:

'Start the engine.'

Maigret turned to Judel.

'Do you have their statements?'

'Yes. They've both signed. In any case, they'll be spending at least four days unloading on Quai de l'Arsenal.'

That was just over two kilometres downstream, between the Bastille and the Seine.

It took some time to get the boat moving, as its bilge was too full and kept scraping the bottom, but at last it was in the lock, and the gates were closed.

Most of the onlookers were starting to move away. Those who remained had nothing to do and would probably be there all day.

Victor hadn't taken off his rubber suit.

'If there are other pieces,' he said, 'they're further upstream. The thighs, the trunk, the head – they're all heavier than an arm and are less likely to be dragged along.'

No current was visible on the surface of the canal, and the rubbish floating on it seemed motionless.

'There isn't a current like in a river, of course. But with every sluice, the water moves almost invisibly all along the reach.'

'So we'd have to search all the way to the next lock?'

'The authorities pay, and you give the orders,' Victor said, puffing at his cigarette.

'Will it take long?'

'It depends where I find the rest of him. That's if the rest of him is in the canal, obviously!'

Why would part of the body have been thrown in the canal and the rest on a patch of waste ground, for example?

'Carry on.'

Cadet signalled to his assistant to moor the boat a little further upstream and got ready to put the brass helmet on again.

Maigret took Judel and Lapointe aside. They formed a little group on the quayside, and the onlookers watched them with the respect people unconsciously show to those in official positions.

'Just in case, you should have the waste grounds and building sites in the area searched thoroughly.'

'I already thought of that,' Judel said. 'I was just waiting for your instructions to start.'

'How many men do you have?'

'This morning, two. By this afternoon, I can have three.'

'Try to find out if there have been any fights locally in the last few days, if anyone heard any screams, calls for help.'

'Yes, chief.'

Maigret left the uniformed officer to keep watch on the human arm that still lay on the quayside under a tarpaulin.

'Coming, Lapointe?'

He walked to Popaul's, the bar on the corner, which was painted a bright red, and opened the glass door. A number of factory workers from the area, already in their work clothes, were having a bite to eat at the counter.

'What can I get you?' the owner hastened to ask.

'Do you have a telephone?'

As he spoke, he saw it. It was attached to the wall, not in a booth but right next to the counter.

'Come on, Lapointe.'

He had no desire to make a call in public.

'Aren't you having a drink?'

Popaul looked offended.

'Later,' Maigret promised him.

All along the quayside there were one-storey houses, as well as apartment blocks, workshops and big concrete buildings containing offices.

'We're bound to find a bistro with a phone booth.'

They continued on their way. On the other side of the canal, the faded flag and blue lamp of the police station came into view, with the dark mass of the Hôpital Saint-Louis behind it.

They walked almost 300 metres before finding a dim-looking bistro. Maigret pushed open the door. They had to go down two stone steps. The floor consisted of little dark-red tiles, the kind found in buildings in Marseille.

There was nobody in the room, only a big ginger cat lying near the stove. It rose lazily, padded towards a half-open door and disappeared.

'Is there anyone here?' Maigret called.

They could hear the rapid ticking of a cuckoo clock. The air smelled of brandy and white wine, brandy more than wine, with a whiff of coffee.

There was movement in a back room. A woman's voice said, with a touch of weariness:

'Just coming!'

The ceiling was low and smoke-dulled, the walls blackened, the room shrouded in a semi-darkness crossed by a few sunbeams, like the light through stained-glass windows in a church. There was a piece of cardboard stuck to the wall, on which were the words, roughly written:

Light meals throughout the day

And, on another notice:

Customers may bring their own food

Right now, nobody seemed tempted by this proposition. Maigret and Lapointe were probably the first customers of the day. There was a phone booth in a corner. Maigret wouldn't go to it until the woman appeared.

When at last she arrived, she was just finishing sticking pins in her dark brown, almost black hair. She was thin and ageless, forty or forty-five perhaps, and she came towards them with a glum expression on her face, her felt slippers dragging over the tiles.

'What do you want?'

Maigret looked at Lapointe.

'Is the white wine good?'

She shrugged.

'Two glasses of white wine. Do you have a telephone token?'

He went and shut himself in the booth and called the prosecutor's office to make his verbal report. The man at the other end of the line was a deputy, and he expressed the same surprise as everyone else on learning that the arm fished out of the canal was a man's.

'There's a diver searching at the moment. He thinks the rest of the body, if it's there at all, is somewhere upstream. I'd like personally for Dr Paul to examine the arm as soon as possible.'

'Can I call you back where you are? I'll try to get hold of him right away and come back to you.'

The number was on the telephone. He gave it to the deputy and walked back to the counter, where two glasses had been poured.

'Cheers!' he said, turning to the woman.

She didn't appear to have heard him. She was looking at them without any friendliness, waiting for them to go so that she could return to whatever it was she had been doing, most likely getting dressed.

She must have been pretty once. At least, like everyone, she had been young. Now her eyes, her mouth, her whole body exuded weariness. Could it be that she was ill and waiting for her next attack? Some people who know that at a particular hour they are going to start suffering again have that expression, subdued and yet tense, like drug addicts waiting for the hour of their dose.

'I'm expecting a phone call,' Maigret said as if to apologize.

It was a public place, of course, like all bars and cafés, a place that was somehow anonymous, and yet they both had the impression that they were intruding, that they had arrived somewhere they didn't belong.

'Your wine's good.'

It was true. Most bistros in Paris advertise a 'locally produced wine', but more often than not it's a doctored wine straight from the warehouses at Bercy. This one, though, had a distinctive flavour that Maigret was trying to identify.

'Sancerre?' he asked.

'No. It comes from a little village near Poitiers.'

That was why it had an aftertaste of flint.

'Do you have family there?'

She didn't reply, and Maigret admired the way she was able to remain motionless, looking at them in silence, with no expression on her face. The cat had come to join her and rubbed against her bare legs.

'Where's your husband?'

'As it happens, he's gone to get some.'

Get some wine, was what she meant. It wasn't easy to maintain the conversation. Just as Maigret was motioning to her to refill the glasses, the telephone came to his rescue.

'Yes, speaking. Did you get hold of Paul? . . . Is he free? . . . In an hour? Good, I'll be there.'

What he heard next made him pull a face. The deputy was telling him that the case had been entrusted to Judge Coméliau, almost Maigret's personal enemy, the fussiest, most conformist magistrate in the prosecutor's office.

'He's expressly asked you to keep him informed.'

'I know.'

That meant that Maigret would receive five or six telephone calls from Coméliau every day, and that he would have to go to his office every morning to bring him up to date.

'All right,' he sighed. 'We'll do our best!'

'It's not my fault, inspector. He was the only judge available and . . .'

The sunbeam had moved slightly and now hit Maigret's glass.

'Let's go!' he said, taking money from his pocket. 'What do I owe you?'

And once they were outside:

'Did you bring the car?'

'Yes. It's parked near the lock.'

The wine had put colour in Lapointe's cheeks, and his eyes were a little shiny. From where they were, they could see a group of onlookers on the quayside watching the diver's movements. When Maigret and the inspector came level with them, Victor's assistant pointed to a package lying on the deck of the boat, a bulkier package than the first one.

'A leg and a foot,' he said, spitting in the water.

The wrapping was less damaged than with the first discovery, and Maigret didn't feel the need to examine it closely.

'Do you think it's worth calling for a van?' he asked Lapointe.

'There must be room in the boot.'

The idea didn't appeal to either of them, but nor did they want to keep Dr Paul waiting. He was expecting them at the Forensic Institute, a bright modern building on the banks of the Seine, not far from the place where the canal joins the river.

'What shall I do?' Lapointe asked.

Maigret preferred to say nothing. Overcoming his revulsion, Lapointe carried the two packages, one after the other, to the boot of the car.

'Do they smell?' Maigret asked him when he returned to the quayside.

And Lapointe, who was holding his hands away from his body, wrinkled his nose and nodded.

Dr Paul was in his white coat and rubber gloves, chain smoking. He liked to say that tobacco is one of the most reliable antiseptics, and in the course of a post-mortem he sometimes got through two whole packets of cigarettes.

Bent over the marble table, working with enthusiasm and even good humour, he spoke between puffs on his cigarette.

'Of course, nothing I can tell you now is final. First of all, I'd like to see the rest of the body, which will tell us more than an arm and a leg, and secondly, before I express a firm opinion, I'd need to run a number of tests.'

'How old?'

'As far as I can judge at first sight, the man must have been between fifty and sixty, closer to fifty than sixty. Look at this hand.'

'What am I looking for?'

'It's a wide, strong hand which must have done heavy manual work at some time.'

'A factory worker.'

'No. More likely a farm labourer. I'd wager, though, that it's been many years since this hand last held a heavy tool. The man didn't exactly look after himself, as you can see from the nails, especially the toenails.'

'A tramp?'

'I don't think so. I repeat: I'd need to see the rest, if it's found, before I could state a firm opinion.'

'How long ago did he die?'

'Again, this is just a hypothesis. Don't get carried away, I might tell you the opposite tonight or tomorrow. For the moment, I'd say three days, no more than that. And I'd be tempted to say less.'

'Not last night?'

'No. But the night before last, maybe.'

Maigret and Lapointe were also smoking, avoiding looking down at the marble slab as far as possible. Dr Paul, though, seemed to enjoy his work, handling his tools with the skill of a conjuror.

He was about to get back into his everyday clothes when Maigret was called to the telephone. It was Judel, from Quai de Valmy.

'They've found the torso!' he announced, sounding quite excited.

'Not the head?'

'Not yet. Victor says that may be more difficult. The weight will have sunk it deeper in the sludge. He also found an empty wallet and a woman's handbag.'

'Near the trunk?'

'No. Quite far. There doesn't seem to be any connection. Like he says, every time he dives in the canal, he could bring enough things up to the surface to start a stall at the flea market. Just before finding the trunk, he brought up a metal bedstead and two wash-basins.'

Paul was waiting before taking his gloves off, holding his hands apart.

'Something new?' he asked.

Maigret nodded. Then, to Judel:

'Can you get it to me at the Forensic Institute?'

'Possibly . . .'

'I'll wait here. Make it quick, because Dr Paul . . .'

They waited in the main doorway, where the air was cooler and more pleasant and from where they could watch the constant bustle on Pont d'Austerlitz. On the other side of the Seine, some barges and a little sea-going boat were unloading goods outside the bonded warehouses. There was something young, something lively, in the rhythm of Paris this morning. A season was starting, a brand-new spring, and people were optimistic.

'No tattoos or scars, I assume?'

'Not on the parts I've examined, no. From his skin, I'd say he was a man who lived indoors.'

'He seems quite hairy.'

'Yes. I can almost describe to you the kind of person he was. Dark-skinned, not very tall, short but stocky, with bulging muscles, thick dark hair on the arms, hands, legs and chest. The French countryside produces lots of people like that: sturdy, wilful, stubborn. I'm curious to see his head.'

'When we find it!'

A quarter of an hour later, two uniformed officers brought them the trunk. Dr Paul was almost rubbing his hands as he walked to the marble slab like a cabinetmaker to his work bench.

'This confirms we aren't dealing with a professional job,' he muttered. 'I mean the man wasn't cut up by a butcher, or by a specialist from La Villette, let alone a surgeon! For the bones, an ordinary metal saw was used. For the rest, they seem to have used a big carving knife, the kind that's found in restaurants and in most kitchens. It must have taken a while. They had to start again several times.'

He paused.

'Look at this hairy chest . . .'

Maigret and Lapointe merely glanced at it.

'No obvious wounds?'

'I can't see any. What's certain, of course, is that the man didn't die from drowning.'

It was almost funny. The idea that a man whose body parts had been found in the canal might have actually drowned . . .

'I'll look at the internal organs later, in particular, in so far as I can, the stomach contents. Are you staying?'

Maigret shook his head. It wasn't a spectacle he particularly enjoyed, and he was in urgent need of a drink, not wine this time, but something a lot stronger, to get rid of the bad taste he had in his mouth, a taste he thought of as a corpse taste.

'Hold on a bit, Maigret . . . What was I saying? . . . You see this lighter line, and these small pale spots on the stomach?'

Maigret said yes without looking.

'The line is the scar left by an operation performed several years ago. An operation for appendicitis.'

'And the spots?'

'That's the oddest thing. I can't swear I'm right, but I'm almost sure they're marks left by shotgun pellets. That would confirm that the man lived in the countryside at some time in his life, a farm labourer or a gamekeeper, something like that. A long time ago, twenty years, maybe more, he must have been fired at with a shotgun. I count seven . . . no, eight scars of the same kind, in a rainbow arc. I've only seen that once before, and it wasn't as regular. I'll have to take a photograph of it for my records.'

'Will you phone me?'

'Where will you be? At headquarters?'

'Yes, in my office. And I'll probably have lunch on Place Dauphine.'

'I'll call you and let you know what I've discovered.'

Once they were outside, in the sun, Maigret was the first to wipe his forehead. Lapointe was unable to stop himself from spitting several times as if he, too, had an acrid taste in his mouth.

'I'll have the boot of the car disinfected as soon as we get to headquarters,' he said.

Before getting in the car, they went into a bistro and had a glass of marc. It was so strong that Lapointe retched and held his hand in front of his mouth for a moment, his eyes filled with anxiety, wondering if he wasn't going to vomit.

At last he regained his composure.

'I beg your pardon,' he stammered.

As they were going out, the owner of the bar said to one of his customers:

'More people who came to identify a body. They all react like that.'

Located as he was just opposite the Forensic Institute, he was used to it.

2. The Bottle Wax

For a brief moment, as Maigret entered the main corridor at Quai des Orfèvres, a gleam of gaiety played on his eyes, because today even this corridor, the greyest and grimmest on earth, was touched by the sun, at least in the form of a kind of luminous dust.

Between the doors of the offices, people were waiting on backless benches, some with their wrists handcuffed. He was about to head for the commissioner's office to bring him up to date with the discoveries at Quai de Valmy when a man stood up and touched the brim of his hat by way of greeting.

With the familiarity of people who have been seeing each other every day for years, Maigret said:

'Well, viscount, what do you think of this? You're always complaining that it's only prostitutes who are cut up into pieces . . .'

The man everybody called the viscount did not blush, even though he had probably understood the allusion. He was a homosexual, a discreet one, admittedly. He had been 'doing' Quai des Orfèvres for more than fifteen years for a Paris newspaper, a press agency and some twenty provincial dailies.

He was the last person to still dress the way people dressed in drawing-room comedies from the beginning of the century, and a monocle hung from a broad black ribbon over his chest. Perhaps it was because of that monocle, which he almost never used, that he had been given his nickname?

'So they haven't found the head yet?'

'Not as far as I know.'

'I've just phoned Judel, who says they haven't. If you hear anything more, inspector, don't forget me.'

He went and sat down again on his bench while Maigret continued on his way to the commissioner's office. The window of the office was open, and from here, too, barges could be seen moving along the Seine. The two men spoke for about ten minutes.

When Maigret opened the door to his own office, a note was waiting for him on the blotting pad, and he knew immediately who it was from. As expected, it was a message from Judge Coméliau asking him to phone him as soon as he arrived.

'Detective Chief Inspector Maigret here, sir.'

'Hello, there, Maigret. Have you just come from the canal?'

'From the Forensic Institute.'

'Is Dr Paul there?'

'He's working on the organs as we speak.'

'I don't suppose the body has been identified yet?'

'We can hardly count on it in the absence of the head. Unless we have a stroke of luck . . .'

'Actually, that's what I wanted to talk to you about. In an ordinary case, where the victim's identity is known, we know more or less where we're going. Are you following me? In this case, on the contrary, we have no idea who we may be dealing with tomorrow, the day after tomorrow or in an hour. Anything is possible, even the most unpleasant of surprises, and we have to be extremely cautious.'

Coméliau enunciated his words carefully, as if listening to the sound of his own voice. Everything he did, everything he said, was 'extremely' important.

Most examining magistrates practically never take over a case until the police have sorted it out. Coméliau, on the other hand, insisted on being in charge of operations as soon as the investigation started, which may have been due above all to his fear of complications. His brother-in-law was a prominent politician, one of those rare parliamentarians who had been involved in almost all the ministries.

'As I'm sure you'll understand,' Coméliau liked to say, 'because of him my situation is more delicate than that of any other magistrate.'

Eventually, Maigret got away with a promise to call him every time there was the slightest new development, even at home in the evening. He went through his mail, looked in on the inspectors' office and sent some of them off in connection with a number of current cases.

'Today is Tuesday, isn't it?'

'Yes, chief.'

If Dr Paul's first estimate had been correct, and the body had been in the Canal Saint-Martin for about forty-eight hours, that meant the murder had taken place on Sunday, or probably Saturday night, because it wasn't very likely that somebody would have thrown in those sinister packages in broad daylight, less than 500 metres from a police station.

'Is that you, Madame Maigret?' he said to his wife in a jokey tone when he had her at the other end of the line. 'I won't be back for lunch. What had you made?'

Lamb and bean stew. He didn't have any regrets: it was too heavy for a day like today.

He called Judel.

'Anything new?'

'Right now, Victor is having a bite to eat on board his boat. We now have the whole body apart from the head. He's asking if he should continue his search.'

'Of course.'

'My men are at work, but don't yet have anything specific. There was a fight on Sunday evening in a bar in Rue des Récollets. Not at Popaul's. Further away, near Faubourg Saint-Martin. There's a concierge complaining that her husband is missing, but he hasn't been home for a month, and the description doesn't match.'

'I'll probably be over there this afternoon.'

On his way out to lunch at the Brasserie Dauphine, he opened the door to the inspectors' office.

'Coming, Lapointe?'

It struck him, as they were walking beside the river in silence, that he didn't really need the young inspector in order to eat at his usual table in the little restaurant on Place Dauphine. A smile hovered over his lips at the memory of a question he had been asked about this. It was his friend Pardon, the doctor in Rue Popincourt he had got into the habit of having dinner with once a month with his wife, who had asked him in a perfectly serious tone one evening:

'Could you tell me, Maigret, why plainclothes policemen always go around in twos, just like plumbers?'

It had never struck him before, and he had to admit that it was true. He himself rarely handled an investigation without being accompanied by one of his inspectors.

He had scratched his head.

'I suppose the first reason goes back to the time when the streets of Paris weren't safe and it was better to be with someone rather than alone when you ventured into certain neighbourhoods, especially at night.'

That remained valid in some cases, in that of an arrest, for example, or a raid on some seedy premises or other. All the same, Maigret had continued to give it some thought.

'There is a second reason, which also holds true for interrogations at Quai des Orfèvres. If only one police officer takes a testimony, the suspect, who might have talked reluctantly, can always deny his confession subsequently. Two statements have more weight than one in front of a jury.'

That made sense, but he still hadn't been satisfied.

'From a practical point of view, it's almost a necessity. During a stakeout, for example, you may need to make a phone call without taking your eyes off the person you're watching. Or the person may have gone into a building with several exits.'

Pardon, who was also smiling, had objected:

'Whenever I'm given several reasons, I tend to think that none of them is sufficient by itself.'

To which Maigret had replied:

'In that case, I'll speak for myself. The reason I almost always make sure I'm accompanied by an inspector is because, if I was on my own, I'd be afraid of getting bored.'

He didn't tell this story to Lapointe, because you should never display scepticism in front of the young, and Lapointe still burned with zeal. The lunch was pleasant and quiet, with other inspectors and detective chief inspectors standing at the bar, four or five eating in the restaurant.

'Do you think the head was thrown in the canal? Will we find it?'

Maigret caught himself shaking his head. Actually, he hadn't yet thought about it. His response was instinctive. He would have been incapable of saying why he had the impression that Victor the diver would search in vain through the sludge of the Canal Saint-Martin.

'What could they have done with it?'

He had no idea. Maybe deposit it, inside a suitcase, in the left luggage office at Gare de l'Est, which was quite close, for example, or Gare du Nord, which wasn't much further away. Or else send it to some address in the provinces in one of those huge express lorries he had seen parked in one of the streets leading to Quai de Valmy. He had often seen those red and green lorries crossing the city in the direction of the main roads and he had never known where they had their home base. It was right there, near the canal, in Rue Terrage. At a certain point during the morning, he had counted more than twenty of them parked at the kerb, all bearing the words 'Zenith Transport: Roulers and Langlois'.

This indicated that he wasn't thinking about anything in particular. The case interested him without fascinating him. His interest came above all from the fact that he hadn't worked in the area of the canal for a long time. There was a period, early in his career, when every one of the streets in the neighbourhood had been familiar to him, as well as a good many of the figures creeping past the houses at night.

They were still at the table, having coffee, when Maigret was called to the telephone. It was Judel.

'I don't know if I did the right thing disturbing you, chief. It's not exactly a lead yet. About an hour ago, one of my men, Blancpain, who I put on guard duty near the diver's boat, noticed a boy on a delivery tricycle. He thought he'd already seen him in the morning, then half an hour later, and so on, several times throughout the morning. Other onlookers stayed on the quayside for a while, but this one, according to Blancpain, kept his distance and seemed more interested than the others. Usually, a delivery boy has his rounds to do and no time to waste.'

'Did Blancpain question him?'

'He intended to. He walked up to him as calmly as possible in order not to scare him. He'd only gone a few metres when the young man, giving every indication that he was scared, jumped on his tricycle and sped off in the direction of Rue des Récollets. Blancpain didn't have a car or any means of transport at his disposal. He tried in vain to catch up with the fugitive, while passers-by turned to

29

look at him and the tricycle vanished in the traffic on Faubourg Saint-Martin.'

The two men fell silent. Obviously, it was flimsy. It might mean nothing, but equally it might constitute a point of departure.

'Does Blancpain have his description?'

'Yes. The young man was between eighteen and twenty, and looked like he's from the country, to judge by his ruddy face. He had long fair hair and was wearing a leather jacket over a roll-neck sweater. Blancpain couldn't read the word on the delivery tricycle. A word ending in "ail". We're just checking the list of local merchants who might use a delivery boy on a tricycle.'

'What does Victor say?'

'That as long as he's paid, he doesn't care if he's in the water or out of it, but he's convinced he's wasting his time.'

'Nothing on the patches of waste ground?'

'Not so far.'

'I hope to have a few details on the dead man soon, when I get the pathologist's report.'

He received them in his office, about 2.30, by telephone. Paul would send him his official report later.

'Are you taking notes, Maigret?'

Maigret drew a pad towards him.

'These are just estimates, but they're quite close to reality. First of all, here's a description of your man, in so far as it can be established without the head. He isn't tall: about 1 metre 67. The neck is short and thick, and I have reason to think the face is broad, with a solid jaw. Dark hair, with perhaps some white hair at the temples, not much. Weight: 75 kilos. He was probably a thickset man, more square than round, more muscular than fat, though he's put on weight recently. The liver indicates a regular drinker, though I don't think we're dealing with a drunk. More likely the sort who has a drink every hour or half-hour, especially white wine. In fact, I found traces of white wine in the stomach.'

'Food, too?'

'Yes. We're lucky it was something hard to digest. His last lunch or dinner consisted mostly of roast pork and beans.'

'How long before his death?'

'I'd say between two and two and a half hours. I lifted the material under his fingernails and toenails and sent it to the lab. Moers will give you his verdict himself.'

'What about scars?'

'I haven't changed my opinion from this morning. The appendectomy was performed five or six years ago, by a good surgeon to judge by the quality of the work. The marks from shotgun pellets date from at least twenty years ago, and I'm tempted to double that figure.'

'How old?'

'Fifty to fifty-five.'

'So he would have been fired at with a shotgun when he was a child?'

'That's my opinion. General health satisfactory, apart from the clogging of the liver that I mentioned. Heart and lungs in good condition. The left lung bears the scar of a very old and mild bout of tuberculosis. Children or babies sometimes have a mild bout of tuberculosis without even noticing. Now, Maigret, if you want more than this, bring me the head and I'll do what I can.'

'They haven't found it.'

'In that case, they won't.'

He confirmed Maigret in his opinion. At Quai des Orfèvres, there are a certain number of beliefs that have ended up being considered axiomatic. One is that it's almost invariably low-class prostitutes who are cut into pieces. Another is that a certain number of pieces might be found, but more rarely the head.

No one can back it up, but everyone believes it.

He went into the inspectors' office.

'If anyone calls me,' he said, 'I'm upstairs in the lab.'

He slowly climbed to the upper floors of the Palais de Justice, where he found Moers bent over test tubes.

'Are you working on "my" corpse?' he asked.

'I'm studying the specimens Paul sent us.'

'Any results?'

Other specialists were working in the huge room, where, in a corner, stood the tailor's dummy that was used for reconstructions, for example to check that a blow with a knife could only have been delivered from such and such an angle.

'I have the impression,' murmured Moers, who always spoke in a low voice, as if in a church, 'that your man didn't get out much.'

'Why?'

'I've examined the material extracted from the toenails, which means I can tell you that the last socks he wore were navy blue wool. I've also found traces of the kind of felt they make carpet slippers from. From which I conclude that the man must have spent a lot of his time in his slippers.'

'If that's correct, Paul should be able to confirm it, because living in slippers for years ends up deforming the foot, at least if I'm to believe my wife, who's always telling me . . .'

He didn't finish his sentence. He tried the Forensic Institute, was told that Dr Paul had left and managed to get hold of him at home.

'This is Maigret. One question, doctor, based on something Moers just told me. Do you have the impression that our man spent more time in slippers than in shoes?'

'Congratulate Moers for me. I almost mentioned it earlier but I thought it was a bit flimsy and might have ended up as a false lead. It occurred to me, when I examined the feet, that we might be dealing with a waiter. In waiters, especially head waiters, and in . . . well, in policemen, traffic cops in particular, the soles of the feet tend to collapse, not because of walking a lot but because of standing a lot.'

'You told me the fingernails weren't well looked after.'

'That's right. Most likely, a head waiter wouldn't leave his nails in such a bad state.'

'Or a waiter in a respectable café or restaurant.'

'Has Moers discovered anything else?'

'Not so far. Thank you, doctor.'

Maigret spent almost another half an hour prowling the lab, peering over everyone's shoulders.

'It may interest you to know that he also had a mixture of earth and saltpetre under his nails.'

Moers knew as well as Maigret where such a mixture was most often found: in cellars, especially damp cellars.

'Is there a little? A lot?'

'That's what strikes me. The man doesn't seem to have dirtied himself like that on only one occasion.'

'In other words, he was in the habit of going down into a cellar?'

'It's only a hypothesis.'

'And the hands?'

'I've found similar material under the fingernails, but mixed with something else, small fragments of red wax.'

'Like the kind used to seal bottles of wine?'

'Yes.'

Maigret was almost disappointed: this was becoming too easy.

'In other words, a bistro!' he muttered.

At that moment, he wondered if the case might not be wrapped up by this evening. The image of the thin, brown-haired woman who had served them their drinks this morning came back into his mind. He had been very struck by her and had thought two or three times about her during the day, not necessarily in connection with the dismembered man, but because she was no ordinary character.

There was no lack of colourful individuals in a neighbourhood like Quai de Valmy. But he had seldom encountered the kind of inertia he had seen in that woman.

It was hard to explain. When most people look at you, there is some sort of exchange, however small. A contact is established, even if that contact is a kind of defiance.

With her, on the contrary, there was nothing. She had shown no surprise, no fear as she served them; her face was unreadable, displaying nothing but a weariness that probably never left her.

Unless it was indifference?

Two or three times, while drinking his wine, Maigret had looked into her eyes and had discovered nothing, had provoked no flicker, no reaction.

This wasn't the passivity of an unintelligent person. She wasn't drunk either, or on drugs, at least at the time. Already that morning, he had vowed to go back and see her, if only to get an idea of the kind of customers who frequented the establishment.

'Any ideas, chief?'

'Maybe.'

'You say that as if it bothered you.'

Maigret preferred not to insist. At four o'clock, he summoned Lapointe, who was busy with paperwork.

'Do you mind driving me?'

'To the canal?'

'Yes.'

'I hope they've had time to disinfect the car.'

The women were already wearing light-coloured hats, and this season it was red that dominated, a bright poppy red. The striped or orange awnings had been lowered on the café terraces, where almost all the tables were occupied, and people had more of a spring in their step than a week earlier.

When they reached Quai de Valmy, they got out of the car close to where the crowd stood, indicating the place where Victor was still searching the bottom of the canal. Judel was there.

'Anything?'

'No.'

'No clothes either?'

'We looked at the string. If you think it's useful, I'll send some to the lab. At first sight, it's ordinary thick string, the kind used by most shopkeepers. It took quite a bit of it to make the different packages. I sent someone to question the local ironmongers. So far, no results. As for the newspaper, I put out the scraps to dry. Most are from last week.'

'When's the last one from?'

'Saturday morning.'

'Do you know the bistro that's just past Rue Terrage, next to a pharmaceuticals laboratory?'

'Calas'?'

'I didn't look at the name above the door: a dark little room, below street level, with a big coal stove in the middle and a black pipe crossing almost the whole room.'

'Yes, that's Omer Calas' place.'

The local inspectors knew these places better than the people from headquarters.

'What kind of place is it?' Maigret asked, watching the bubbles that indicated Victor's comings and goings at the bottom of the canal.

'Quiet. I don't remember them ever being in trouble with us.'

'Is Omer Calas from the country?'

'Quite likely. I could check in the registers. Most bistro owners arrive in Paris as manservants or chauffeurs, marry the cook and eventually set up in business for themselves.'

'Have they been there for a long time?'

'They were there before I was assigned to the neighbourhood. I've always known the place as you've seen it. It's almost opposite the police station, and I sometimes cross the footbridge and have a glass of white wine there. Their white wine's good.'

'Is the owner usually behind the counter?'

'Most of the time. Except for part of the afternoon, when he goes and plays billiards in a brasserie in Rue La Fayette. He's crazy about billiards.'

'Does his wife serve when he's away?'

'Yes. They don't have a maid or a waiter. I seem to remember they did have a girl who helped out for a while, but I don't know what became of her.'

'What kind of customers do they get?'

'Hard to say,' Judel said, scratching the back of his neck. 'The bistros in the area all have more or less similar kinds of customers. And at the same time, they each have a different clientele. Popaul's, for example, near the lock, is busy all day long. A lot of drinking goes on, it's noisy and the air's always blue with smoke. After eight in the evening, you're sure to find three or four women there, and they all have their regulars, too.'

'And Omer's?'

'First of all, not so many people pass by there. Secondly, it's darker, sadder. It's not much fun in there, as you must have noticed. In the morning, they have the workers from the building sites who come in for a drink, and at midday, there are a few who bring their food with them and order a bottle of white wine. The afternoon's quieter because, like I said, not many people pass that way. I suppose that's why Omer chooses that time of day to go and play billiards. Someone probably drops in from time to time. Then just before dinner, people come in for an aperitif and things liven up again.

'I sometimes go in of an evening. Each time I've noticed a table with people playing cards and one or two people, no more than that, standing at the counter. It's the kind of place where, if you're not a regular, you always feel you're disturbing something.'

'Are Omer and the woman married?'

'I've never thought about it. It's easy enough to check. We can go straight to the station and look at the registers.'

'Tell me later. Omer Calas seems to be away right now.'

'Did she tell you that?'

'Yes.'

By now, the Naud brothers' barge was moored at Quai de l'Arsenal, and cranes had started unloading the freestone.

'I'd like a list of the local bistros, especially those where the owner or the waiter has been away since Sunday.'

'You think . . .'

'The idea came from Moers. He may be right. I'm going to take a walk over there.'

'To Calas'?'

'Yes. Are you coming, Lapointe?'

'Shall I ask Victor to come back tomorrow?'

'I think it'd be a waste of taxpayers' money. If he hasn't found anything today, that means there's nothing more to find.'

'That's what he thinks, too.'

'Tell him to knock off when he's had enough. And remind him to send in his report tomorrow.'

Passing Rue Terrage, Maigret glanced at the lorries parked outside a huge gate with the words 'Roulers and Langlois' above it.

'I wonder how many they have,' he said, thinking aloud.

'How many what?' Lapointe asked.

'Lorries.'

'Whenever I go for a drive in the country, I see some on the road. They're a nightmare to overtake.'

The chimney pots were no longer pink, as they had been that morning, but were verging on dark red in the rays of the setting sun, and in the sky there were now traces of pale green, the same green, or almost, that the sea turns to just before sunset.

'Do you think, chief, that a woman would have been capable of doing something like that?'

He was thinking of the thin, brown-haired woman who had served them that morning.

'It's possible. I have no idea.'

Was Lapointe also thinking that would be too easy? When a case proves complicated and the problem appears impossible to solve, everyone at headquarters, starting with Maigret, becomes surly and impatient. Conversely, if a case which has seemed difficult at first turns out to be straightforward and trivial, the same men, including Maigret, are unable to conceal their disappointment.

They had come to the bistro. Because it had a low ceiling, it was darker than the others, and a light had already been switched on over the counter.

The same woman as in the morning, dressed in the same way, was serving two customers who looked like office workers. She didn't react on recognizing Maigret and Lapointe.

'What will it be?' she asked simply, without taking the trouble to smile.

'White wine.'

There were three or four bottles of it, uncorked, in the zinc tub behind the counter. Presumably, it was necessary to go down to the cellar every now and again and refill the bottles straight from the cask. Close to the counter, the floor wasn't covered in red tiles, and a trapdoor about one metre square was visible, giving access to the cellar.

Maigret and Lapointe had not sat down. From the words they heard uttered by the two men standing near them, they guessed that they weren't office workers but male nurses who were about to go on night duty at the Hôpital Saint-Louis on the other side of the canal. After a while, one of them turned to the woman and asked in the familiar tone of a regular:

'When's Omer coming back?'

'You know very well he never tells me.'

She had answered as unconcernedly, as indifferently as when she had spoken to Maigret in the morning. The ginger cat was still by the stove and didn't seem to have moved.

'Apparently they're still looking for the head!' said the man who had asked the question.

As he said this, he leaned forwards to look at Maigret and Lapointe. Had he seen them by the canal? Or did he simply have the impression they were police officers?

'They haven't found it yet, have they?' he continued, addressing Maigret directly.

'Not yet.'

'Do you expect they will?'

The other man was looking at Maigret's face and eventually asked:

'You're Detective Chief Inspector Maigret, aren't you?'

'Yes.'

'I thought as much. I've often seen your picture in the newspapers.'

The woman still hadn't reacted, didn't even seem to have heard.

'It's funny that for once it should be a man who was cut into pieces! Are you coming, Julien? What do I owe you, Madame Calas?'

They left, waving a perfunctory goodbye to Maigret and Lapointe.

'Do you have a lot of customers from among the staff of the hospital?'

'A few,' she simply replied.

'Did your husband leave on Sunday evening?'

She looked at him with expressionless eyes and said in the same indifferent voice:

'Why Sunday?'

'I don't know. I thought I heard someone say—'

'He left on Friday afternoon.'

'Were there a lot of people in the bar when he left?'

She appeared to think this over. She sometimes seemed so absent, or so indifferent to what was being said, that she came across like a sleepwalker.

'There are never many people in the afternoon.'

'Can you recall anybody?'

'There may have been someone. I don't remember. I didn't pay attention.'

'Did he take any luggage with him?'

'Of course.'

'A lot?'

'His suitcase.'

'How was he dressed?'

'He was wearing a grey suit, I think. Yes.'

'Do you know where he is right now?'

'No.'

'Do you have any idea where he went?'

'I know he must have taken the train to Poitiers, and from there, the bus for Saint-Aubin or another village round about.'

'Does he stay at the village inn?'

'Usually, yes.'

'Does he ever stay with friends or relatives? Or with the vineyard owners who supply him with wine?'

'I've never asked him.'

'So if something happened, if you fell ill, for example, and needed to get hold of him urgently, you wouldn't be able to?'

The thought neither surprised nor frightened her.

'He always comes back in the end,' she replied in her flat, monotonous voice. 'Same again?'

The two glasses were empty and she filled them.

3. The Young Man on the Delivery Tricycle

When all was said and done, it was one of Maigret's most disappointing interrogations. In fact, it wasn't an interrogation strictly speaking, since the life of the little bistro went on as usual. For a long time, Maigret and Lapointe stood at the counter, drinking their wine like customers. And in reality, that was what they were: customers. Even though one of the male nurses had recognized Maigret and said his name out loud, Maigret himself, in addressing Madame Calas, made no mention of his official function. He spoke to her from time to time, with long silences between his questions, and she for her part, when he didn't ask her anything, simply ignored him.

She left them alone in the room for a time while she disappeared through a back door she left half open. It must have been the kitchen. She was putting something on the stove. While she was gone, a little old man entered and, clearly a regular, walked straight to a table in the corner and took a box of dominoes from a pigeon-hole.

From the back, she could hear the dominoes he was putting on the table, as if he was preparing to play by himself. When she came back in, she didn't say hello to him, simply poured a pink-coloured aperitif into a glass and went and put it down in front of him.

He was waiting. Only a few minutes went by before

another little old man, so similar to him in type that they might have been brothers, came in and sat down opposite him.

'Am I late?'

'No. I was early.'

Madame Calas filled a glass with another kind of aperitif. All this happened in silence, like a mime. In passing, she flicked a switch which turned on a second light at the far end of the room.

'Doesn't she make you nervous?' Lapointe whispered in Maigret's ear.

It wasn't nervousness that Maigret felt, but interest: it had been a long time since he had last had the opportunity to show such interest in a human being.

When he was young and dreaming of the future, hadn't he imagined an ideal profession which unfortunately doesn't exist in real life? He hadn't told anyone, and never uttered these words aloud, even to himself, but he would have liked to be a 'mender of destinies'.

Curiously, though, in his career as a policeman, he had quite often come across people whom the vicissitudes of life had steered in the wrong direction and he had been able to put them back where they belonged. Even more curiously, in the course of the last few years, a profession had been born that somewhat resembled the one he had imagined: the psychoanalyst, who tries to reveal to people their true personalities.

Well, if anyone clearly wasn't where they belonged, it was this woman who came and went in silence, giving no clue as to her thoughts and feelings.

Admittedly, he had already discovered one of her secrets, if you could call it a secret: her customers probably all knew. Twice more, she had returned to the back room, and the second time she did this, Maigret had clearly heard the squeak of a cork in the neck of a bottle.

She drank. He would have sworn she was never drunk, never lost her self-control. Like true drunks, those for whom medical treatment can do nothing, she knew her limits and kept herself in this resolute state, this kind of somnambulistic indifference that was so intriguing at first glance.

'How old are you?' he asked her when she resumed her place behind the counter.

'Forty-one.'

She hadn't hesitated. She had replied without either pride or bitterness. She knew she looked older than that. She had probably stopped living for other people a long time ago and no longer cared about their opinions. Her face was withered, with deep circles under her eyes, the corners of her mouth sagged, and there were already weak folds under her chin. She must have lost weight, and her dress, too big for her now, hung from her body.

'Born in Paris?'

'No.'

He was sure she guessed what was behind his questions, but she didn't try to avoid them; on the other hand, she didn't use a single word more than was necessary.

Behind Maigret, the two old men were playing their game of dominoes, as they probably did at this time every afternoon.

What bothered Maigret was that she should hide in order to drink. If she didn't care what people thought, what was the point of going into the back room to get a swig of brandy or wine straight from the bottle? Was it because she still retained a degree of self-respect? It seemed unlikely. When drunks get to that point, they rarely bother to hide, unless those around them are constantly keeping an eye on them.

Was that the answer to the question? There was a husband, Omer Calas. Could it be assumed that he prevented his wife from drinking, at any rate in front of the customers?

'Does your husband often go to the Poitiers area to buy wine?'

'Every year.'

'Once?'

'Sometimes twice. It depends.'

'On what?'

'On the wine they're selling.'

'Does he always leave on a Friday?'

'I've never paid attention.'

'Did he mention in advance that he planned to make this trip?'

'Mention it to whom?'

'To you.'

'He never tells me what he plans to do.'

'To the customers, then, or to friends?'

'I have no idea.'

'Were those two here last Friday?'

'Not when Omer left. They don't get here until five.'

Maigret turned to Lapointe.

'Can you phone Gare Montparnasse and find out the times of the afternoon trains for Poitiers? Ask for the station chief.'

Maigret spoke in a low voice. If she had watched his lips, Madame Calas would have guessed the words he was saying, but she didn't bother.

'Ask him to check with the employees, especially at the ticket offices. Give a description of the husband . . .'

The phone booth wasn't at the back of the room, as is usually the case, but near the front window. Lapointe asked for a token and took a few steps towards the glass door. It was quite dark by now and a bluish fog hovered on the other side of the windows. Maigret, who had his back to the street, turned abruptly when he heard Lapointe's hurried steps. He thought he saw a shadowy figure running away outside, a young face that seemed pale and shapeless in the semi-darkness.

Lapointe had turned the door handle and was running in his turn in the direction of La Villette. He hadn't had time to shut the door behind him, and Maigret now stepped forwards and went and stood outside in the middle of the pavement. He could just about make out two figures disappearing into the distance, one chasing the other, but for a time he still heard hurried footsteps on the cobbles.

Lapointe must have thought he had recognized someone through the window. Although Maigret had seen almost nothing, he was sure he knew what had happened. The young man who had run away resembled the description of the young man with the delivery tricycle who, while Victor was working at the bottom of the canal, had already run away once before when a police officer approached him.

'Do you know him?' he asked Madame Calas.

'Who?'

There was no point insisting. In any case, it was quite possible she hadn't looked towards the street at the right moment.

'Is it always so quiet here?'

'It depends.'

'On what?'

'The day. The time.'

As if to prove her right, a siren sounded, indicating the end of the working day in a nearby workshop, and a few minutes later there was a sound like a procession along the street, the door opened and closed and opened again a dozen times, and people sat down at the tables while others, like Maigret, stood at the counter.

In many cases, Madame Calas didn't ask them what they were having and automatically served them their usual drinks.

'Isn't Omer here?'

'No.'

She didn't add:

'He's gone on a trip.'

Or else:

'He left for Poitiers on Friday.'

She simply answered direct questions but didn't go into unnecessary details. Where was she from? He didn't feel able to make even a hypothesis. The years had tarnished her, as if part of her had somehow drained away. Because of the drinking, she lived in a world apart and had only a superficial contact with reality.

'Have you been living here long?'

'In Paris?'

'No. This bistro.'

'Twenty-four years.'

'Did your husband own it before he met you?'

'No.'

He made a mental calculation.

'So you were seventeen when you met him?'

'I knew him before.'

'How old is he now?'

'Forty-seven.'

That didn't quite match the age given by Dr Paul, but the margin wasn't as great as all that. Maigret continued to ask questions, but without much conviction, more to satisfy his personal curiosity than anything else. Wouldn't it have been a miracle if, on the very first day, chance had led to his discovering the identity of the headless corpse without his having to make any effort?

There was a murmur of conversation, and a thick layer of cigarette smoke began to drift over everyone's heads. People left. Others came in. The two domino players remained as imperturbable as if they were alone in the world.

'Do you have a photograph of your husband?'

'No.'

'You don't have a single picture of him?'

'No.'

'Or of yourself?'

'Not of myself either. Except on my identity card.'

Maigret knew from experience that people not having a photograph of themselves didn't happen once in a thousand times.

'Do you live upstairs?'

She nodded. The building, he had noted from outside, had only one upper floor. There must be two or three rooms up there, probably two bedrooms and a bathroom or a junk room.

'How do you get up there?'

'There's a staircase from the kitchen.'

She went to the kitchen a little while later, this time to stir something that was cooking. The main door burst open, and Lapointe came in, panting, his cheeks flushed, his eyes shining, pushing a young man in front of him.

Lapointe, the youngest and newest of Maigret's inspectors, had never been so proud of himself.

'He really gave me a run for my money!' he said with a smile, reaching for his drink, which was still on the counter. 'Two or three times, I thought he was going to get away. It's a good thing I was the 500 metre champion at school.'

The young man was also panting heavily.

'I haven't done anything,' he proclaimed, turning to Maigret.

'In that case you have nothing to fear.'

Maigret looked at Lapointe.

'Did you get his identity card?'

'To be on the safe side, I've kept it in my pocket. He's definitely the one who rides a delivery tricycle for a firm called Pincemail. He's also the one who was on the quayside this morning and hurried away when he was approached.'

'Why?' Maigret asked the young man.

The latter had a stubborn air about him. He was the kind of youth who likes to make out that he's tough.

'Why don't you answer?'

'I have nothing to say.'

'Did you get anything from him on the way back?' Maigret asked Lapointe.

'We were too breathless to talk much. His name's Antoine Cristin. He's eighteen and lives with his mother in an apartment in Rue du Faubourg Saint-Martin.'

A few of the customers were looking at them, but not with any unusual degree of curiosity: it wasn't rare in this neighbourhood for the police to put in an appearance.

'What were you doing outside?'

'Nothing.'

'He was looking in through the window,' Lapointe said. 'As soon as I saw him, I remembered what Judel told us, and I rushed outside.'

'Why did you run away if you weren't doing anything wrong?'

The young man hesitated, made sure that at least two of their neighbours were listening and said, lips quivering:

'Because I don't like coppers.'

'But you watch them through the window?'

'There's no law against it.'

'How did you know we were here?'

'I didn't.'

'Then why did you come?'

He blushed and bit his lip, which was thick.

'Answer me.'

'I was passing.'

'Do you know Omer?'

'I don't know anyone.'

'How about Omer's wife?'

Madame Calas was back behind the counter and watching them. Once again, it was impossible to read the slightest fear, the slightest apprehension on her face. If she had something to hide, she was stronger than any culprit or any witness Maigret had ever encountered.

'Do you know her?'

'By sight.'

'Have you ever been in here for a drink?'

'Maybe.'

'Where's your tricycle?'

'With my boss. I finish work at five.'

Maigret signalled to Lapointe. The inspector understood, because it was one of the few agreed signals among the men of the Police Judiciaire. Lapointe went into the phone booth and called, not Gare Montparnasse, but the police station that was almost opposite, on the other side of the canal. He finally managed to get Judel on the line.

'The boy's here, at Calas'. In a few minutes, the chief will let him go, but he'd like someone to be ready to keep a tail on him. Anything new?'

'More false leads and dead ends: fights in four or five bars on Sunday evening; someone who thinks he heard a body fall in the water; a prostitute who claims an Arab stole her handbag . . .'

'Talk to you later.'

Maigret was still beside the young man, feigning indifference.

'What are you drinking, Antoine? Wine? Beer?'

'Nothing.'

'Don't you ever drink?'

'Not with coppers. You're going to have to let me go in the end.'

'You seem very sure of yourself.'

'I know the law.'

He was big-boned, a sturdy country boy who hadn't yet lost his health in Paris. How many times had Maigret seen kids of the same kind end up knocking an old tobacconist or haberdasher senseless for a few hundred francs one evening?

'Do you have brothers and sisters?'

'I'm an only child.'

'Does your father live with you?'

'He's dead.'

'Does your mother work?'

'She's a cleaner.'

'Give him back his identity card,' Maigret said to Lapointe. 'Does it have the right address on it?'

'Yes.'

The boy wasn't yet sure this wasn't a trap.

'Can I go?'

'Whenever you want.'

He didn't say thank you or goodbye, but Maigret surprised a furtive wink he gave Madame Calas.

'Now phone the station.'

He ordered two more glasses of white wine. The bistro had partly emptied. Apart from him and Lapointe, there were only five customers left, including the domino players.

'I don't suppose you know him?'

'Who?'

'The young man who just left.'

'Yes!' she replied without hesitation.

It was so simple that Maigret was thrown.

'Does he come here often?'

'Quite often.'

'For a drink?'

'He doesn't drink much.'

'Beer?'

'And wine sometimes.'

'Is it after his work that you see him?'

'No.'

'During the day?'

She nodded. Her unchanging calm was finally starting to exasperate Maigret.

'When he passes.'

'You mean when he rides by on his tricycle? In other words, when he has deliveries in the area?'

'Yes.'

'Usually around what time?'

'Half past three, four o'clock.'

'Does he have a regular round?'

'I think so.'

'Does he stand at the bar?'

'Sometimes he sits down.'

'Where?'

'At that table there. Near me.'

'Are you good friends?'

'Yes.'

'Why didn't he say that?'

'Probably to act tough.'

'Does he usually act tough?'

'He tries to.'

'Do you know his mother?'

'No.'

'Are you from the same village?'

'No.'

'So he just came in one day, and you became acquainted?'

'Yes.'

'Around half past three, isn't your husband usually in a brasserie playing billiards?'

'Most of the time, yes.'

'Do you think it was by chance that Antoine chose that time to come and see you?'

'It never occurred to me.'

Maigret realized the apparent enormity of the question he was about to ask, but he had a sense things were even more unreal around him.

'Does he flirt with you?'

'That depends on what you mean by that.'

'Is he in love with you?'

'I suppose he likes me.'

'Do you give him presents?'

'I sometimes slip him a banknote from the till.'

'Does your husband know?'

'No.'

'Hasn't he ever noticed?'

'Now and then.'

'Did he get angry?'

'Yes.'

'Did he suspect Antoine?'

'I don't think so.'

When they had gone down the two steps from the entrance, they had entered a world in which all values were different and where words themselves had another meaning. Lapointe was still in the booth, talking to Gare Montparnasse.

'Do you mind my asking you a more personal question, Madame Calas?'

'You'll do what you want to do anyway.'

'Is Antoine your lover?'

She didn't flinch. She didn't turn her eyes away from Maigret.

'Now and then,' she admitted.

'You mean you've had relations with him?'

'You'd have found out in the end. I'm sure it won't take him long to talk.'

'Has it happened often?'

'Quite often.'

'Where?'

The question was of some importance. When Omer

Calas was absent, his wife had to be ready to serve those customers who came in. Maigret glanced up at the ceiling. From the bedroom on the first floor, would she hear the door open and close?

With the same simplicity as ever, she looked towards the far end of the room, the door open on the kitchen.

'In there?'

'Yes.'

'Have you ever been caught?'

'Not by Omer.'

'Who by?'

'A customer once who was wearing shoes with rubber soles and who, on seeing nobody at the counter, headed for the kitchen.'

'Did he say anything?'

'He laughed.'

'Did he tell Omer?'

'No.'

'Did he come back?'

Maigret had an inkling. So far, he hadn't been mistaken about Madame Calas' character, and even his boldest hypotheses had turned out to be correct.

'Did he come back often?' he insisted.

'Two or three times.'

'When Antoine was here?'

'No.'

It was easy to find out if the young man was in the bistro because if he was, and it was before five o'clock, he would have left his tricycle outside the door.

'Were you alone?'

'Yes.'

'Did you have to go with him to the kitchen?'

He had the impression that there was a gleam in her eyes, a barely perceptible irony. Was he mistaken? It seemed to him that, in her silent language, she was saying:

'What's the point of asking me these questions? You've already understood.'

She understood Maigret, too. It was as if they were evenly matched, more precisely as if they both possessed the same experience of life.

It was so quick that a second later Maigret would have sworn it had been a figment of his imagination.

'Are there many others?' he asked in a quieter, almost conspiratorial voice.

'A few.'

Then, without moving, without leaning towards her, he asked a final question:

'Why?'

That was a question she was only able to answer with a vague gesture. She didn't strike a romantic pose, didn't construct a whole novel around herself.

He had asked her why, and if he didn't understand it by himself, she couldn't explain it to him.

But he did understand. It was only a confirmation he was looking for, and she didn't need to speak to give him that.

He knew now how low she had descended. What he still didn't know was where she had started from to get there. Would she reply with the same honesty to questions about her past?

He couldn't test that immediately, because Lapointe now rejoined him.

'There's a train for Poitiers at 4.48 on weekdays,' Lapointe said after a sip of wine. 'The station chief has already questioned two of the employees, but they didn't see anyone answering the description provided. He'll make some more inquiries and give you the result at headquarters. He did say, though, that it might be a better idea to phone Poitiers. As the train stops several times on the way and then continues southwards, fewer passengers get off there than get on at Montparnasse.'

'Pass it on to Lucas. I'd also like him to phone Saint-Aubin and the nearest villages. There must be a constabulary somewhere. There are also the inns.'

Lapointe asked for more tokens, and Madame Calas handed them to him with an indifferent gesture. She didn't ask any questions, seemed to find it natural to be questioned about her husband's travels, even though she knew all about the discovery made in the Canal Saint-Martin and the search that had been going on all day, almost outside her windows.

'Did you see Antoine last Friday?'

'He never comes on Friday.'

'Why?'

'Because he does a different round.'

'But after five o'clock?'

'My husband is almost always back by then.'

'So he didn't come here in the afternoon or in the evening?'

'That's right.'

'And you've been married to Omer Calas for twenty-four years?'

'I've been living with him for twenty-four years.'

'Aren't you married?'

'Yes. We got married at the town hall of the tenth arrondissement, but it's only been sixteen or seventeen years. I'd have to count.'

'Do you have any children?'

'A daughter.'

'Does she live here?'

'No.'

'In Paris?'

'Yes.'

'How old is she?'

'She's just turned twenty-four. I had her when I was seventeen.'

'Is she Omer's daughter?'

'Yes.'

'Definitely?'

'Definitely.'

'Is she married?'

'No.'

'Does she live alone?'

'She has an apartment on the Ile Saint-Louis.'

'Does she work?'

'She's an assistant to one of the surgeons at the Hôtel-Dieu, Professor Lavaud.'

For the first time, she was saying more than was absolutely necessary. Did she still have the same feelings as everybody else, in spite of everything? Was she proud of her daughter?

'Did you see her last Friday?'

'No.'

'Does she ever visit you?'

'Sometimes.'

'When was the last time?'

'About three weeks ago, maybe a month.'

'Was your husband here?'

'I think so.'

'Does your daughter get on well with him?'

'She has as little contact with us as possible.'

'Is she ashamed of you?'

'Maybe.'

'How old was she when she left home?'

Her cheeks had grown slightly flushed.

'Fifteen.'

Her voice was curter than before.

'Without warning?'

She nodded.

'With a man?'

She shrugged.

'I don't know. It makes no difference.'

Only the domino players were still left in the room. They put the dominoes back in the box and tapped the table with coins. Madame Calas knew what they wanted. She went and refilled their glasses.

'Isn't that Maigret?' one of them asked in a low voice.

'Yes.'

'What does he want?'

'He hasn't said.'

She hadn't asked him either. She went to the kitchen, came back to the bar, and murmured:

'If you've finished, it's time I had something to eat.'

'Where do you have your meals?'

'There!' she said, pointing to one of the tables at the back.

'We won't be much longer. Did your husband have appendicitis a few years ago?'

'Five or six years ago. He had an operation.'

'Who performed it?'

'The name will come back to me. Wait. Dr Gran . . . Granvalet. That's the one! He used to live on Boulevard Voltaire.'

'Doesn't he live there any more?'

'He's dead. At least that's what a customer who was also operated on by him told us.'

If Granvalet had been alive, they could have found out from him if Omer Calas bore scars in a rainbow pattern on his stomach. The next day, they would have to try his assistants and the nurses. Unless, of course, Omer had been found alive and well in a village near Poitiers.

'Was your husband fired at with a shotgun some time ago?'

'Not since I've known him.'

'Has he ever gone hunting?'

'Maybe he used to hunt when he lived in the country.'

'You've never noticed some quite faded scars in a rainbow arc on his stomach?'

She seemed to think this over, frowned and finally shook her head.

'Are you sure?'

'I haven't looked at him so closely for a long time.'

'Did you love him?'

'I don't know.'

'How long was he your only lover?'

'Years.'

She had given this word a particular resonance.

'Did you meet when you were very young?'

'We're from the same village.'

'Where's that?'

'A hamlet called Boissancourt, about halfway between Montargis and Gien.'

'Do you ever go back there?'

'No, never.'

'Have you ever been back?'

'No.'

'Is that since you've been with Omer?'

'I was seventeen when I left.'

'Were you pregnant?'

'Six months.'

'Did people know?'

'Yes.'

'Including your parents?'

Still with the same simplicity, which had something incredible about it, she replied curtly:

'Yes.'

'Did you ever see them again?'

'No.'

Lapointe, who had finished giving instructions to Lucas, came out of the booth mopping his brow.

'What do I owe you?' Maigret asked.

She asked her first question:

'Are you going?'

It was his turn to answer with a monosyllable:

'Yes.'

4. The Young Man on the Roof

Maigret had been hesitant to take his pipe from his pocket – something that happened in very few places – and when he had done so, he had assumed the innocent air of someone who automatically keeps his hands busy as he speaks.

Immediately after the briefing in the commissioner's office, which hadn't taken long, and after a conversation with the commissioner by the open window, he had passed through the little door that led from the Police Judiciaire to the prosecutor's office. It was the time of day when almost all the benches were occupied in the corridor where the examining magistrates had their offices, because two black Marias had just arrived in the court-yard. Among the prisoners waiting, handcuffed, between two guards, more than three-quarters were known to Maigret, and a few greeted him as he passed, without any apparent rancour.

Judge Coméliau had telephoned his office two or three times the previous day. He was a thin, wiry man, with a small brown moustache that was probably dyed and the bearing of a cavalry officer. His first words had been:

'Tell me exactly how far you've got.'

Meekly, Maigret had granted his wish, telling him about Victor's successive discoveries at the bottom of the

Canal Saint-Martin and about the head they hadn't yet found. At this point, he had been interrupted.

'I assume the diver is continuing his search today?'

'I didn't think it was necessary.'

'But surely if the trunk and the limbs have been found in the canal, the head can't be far away.'

That was what made relations with him so difficult. He wasn't the only examining magistrate like that, but he was unquestionably the most aggressive. In a sense, he wasn't stupid. A lawyer who had once studied with him claimed that Coméliau had been one of the brightest of his generation.

It had to be assumed that his mind was incapable of grasping certain realities. He came from a very particular, upper-middle-class background with rigid principles and even more sacrosanct taboos, and he couldn't help judging everything according to these principles and these taboos.

Patiently, Maigret explained:

'First of all, sir, Victor knows the canal as well as you know your office and I know mine. He went over the bottom metre by metre, more than two hundred times. He's a conscientious young man. If he says the head isn't there . . .'

'My plumber also knows his job and is also thought of as conscientious. Nevertheless, whenever I send for him, he always starts by telling me it's impossible that anything could be defective in the pipes.'

'In the case of a dismembered corpse, it's unusual for the head to be found in the same place as the body.'

Coméliau was making an effort to understand, looking at Maigret with his sharp little eyes.

'There's a reason for that,' Maigret went on. 'While it's hard to identify severed limbs, especially if they've been in the water for a while, a head is easily recognizable. As it's less bulky than a trunk, it's logical for someone who wants to get rid of it to go to the bother of taking it further away.'

'Let's assume you're right.'

Without appearing to, Maigret had his tobacco pouch in his left hand and was only waiting for a moment's inattention on Coméliau's part to fill his pipe.

He told the magistrate about Madame Calas and described the bar on Quai de Valmy.

'What led you to her?'

'Chance, I admit. I had to make a phone call. In another bar, the telephone was within earshot of everybody, without a booth.'

'Go on.'

He mentioned Calas' departure, the train to Poitiers, Madame Calas' relations with Antoine Cristin, the delivery boy, and the crescent of scars on Calas' body.

'You say this woman claims not to know whether or not her husband had these scars? Do you think she's telling the truth?'

This was beyond Coméliau's understanding, and it angered him.

'To be honest, Maigret, what I don't understand is why you haven't brought this woman and this boy into your office and subjected them to one of those interrogations you're usually so good at. I assume you don't believe a word of her story?'

'That's not necessarily the case.'

'Claiming she doesn't know where her husband went and when he'll be back . . .'

How could someone like Coméliau, who was still living in the Left Bank apartment opposite the Luxembourg where he was born, get an idea of the mentality of Monsieur and Madame Calas?

The trick had worked, though: a match had flared briefly, and Maigret's pipe was lit. Coméliau, who hated tobacco, would glare at him, as he always did whenever anyone was presumptuous enough to smoke in his office, but Maigret was quite determined to maintain his air of innocence.

'It's possible,' he granted, 'that everything she told me is false. It's also possible it's true. We've fished parts of a headless corpse out of the canal. It could be any man between forty-five and fifty-five. So far, there's nothing to identify him. How many men that age have disappeared in the past few days and how many have gone away on a trip without saying exactly where they're going? Should I summon Madame Calas to my office and treat her as a suspect just because she's in the habit of drinking surreptitiously, or because she's having an affair with a young delivery boy who runs away when the police approach him? What would we look like if tomorrow, or in a few hours' time, we discover a head somewhere and it turns out not to be Calas'?'

'Are you keeping an eye on the building?'

'Judel from the tenth arrondissement has put a man on guard duty on the quayside. Last night after dinner, I had another walk around the area.'

'Did you discover anything new?'

'Nothing specific. I questioned a number of prostitutes I came across in the street. The neighbourhood has a completely different atmosphere at night from the way it is in broad daylight. I particularly wanted to know if anyone noticed any suspicious comings and goings around the Calas bistro on Friday evening, or if anyone heard anything.'

'And did they?'

'No, nothing much. But one of the girls did tell me something I haven't yet been able to check. According to her, the Calas woman has another lover, a middle-aged man with red hair who apparently lives or works locally. Admittedly, the girl who told me this is filled with resentment. She claims Madame Calas is hurting all of them. "If at least she got paid for it," she told me, "we wouldn't mind. But with her, it doesn't cost a thing. When men want it, they know where to go. They just have to wait until Calas has his back turned. I haven't been to see for myself, of course, but I'm told she never says no." '

Coméliau sighed painfully on hearing of all this moral turpitude.

'Do as you see fit, Maigret. As far as I'm concerned, it all seems quite clear. And these aren't people who need to be treated with kid gloves.'

'I'll see her again in a while. I'll also see her daughter. Last but not least, I hope to get some information about the identity of the body from the nurses who were present five years ago at Calas' operation.'

Regarding that, there was a curious detail. The previous evening, as he was prowling around the neighbourhood,

Maigret had popped into the bistro, where Madame Calas was sitting on a chair, half asleep, while four men were playing cards. He had asked in which hospital her husband had had his appendix removed.

As far as they knew, Calas was a tough character, a man you wouldn't imagine to be afraid of pain, anxious about his health, obsessed with a fear of dying. He'd only had to undergo a routine operation that was neither serious nor risky.

But instead of going into hospital, he had spent a fairly large sum of money in order to be operated on in a private clinic in Villejuif. Not only was it a private clinic, but it was run by nuns who served as the nurses.

Lapointe was probably there right now and would soon be phoning in his report.

'Don't pussyfoot around, Maigret!' Coméliau said as the inspector got to the door.

It wasn't a question of pussyfooting. Nor was it pity, but that was impossible to explain to someone like Coméliau. From one minute to the next, Maigret had found himself plunged into a world so different from the everyday world that he was having to grope his way. Did the little bistro on Quai de Valmy and its denizens have anything to do with the body thrown into the Canal Saint-Martin? It was possible, just as it was possible the whole thing was a series of coincidences.

He went back to his office. He was starting to assume the glum, surly air that almost always came to him at a certain stage in an investigation. The previous day, he had been making discoveries and storing them away without wondering where they would lead. Now, he was confronted with pieces of the truth and had no idea how to tie them together.

Madame Calas was no longer merely a picturesque character – he had encountered quite a few of those in the course of his career – but a genuine human problem.

To Coméliau, she was a shameless drunk who slept with just anybody.

To him, she was something else, he didn't yet know what exactly, and, as long as he didn't know, as long as he didn't 'feel' the truth, he would remain prey to a vague sense of unease.

Lucas was in his office, putting mail down on the blotting pad.

'Anything new?'

'I didn't know you were around, chief.'

'I was with Coméliau.'

'If I'd known, I would have put the call through to you. There is something new, yes. Judel's in a real state.'

Maigret thought of Madame Calas and wondered what had happened to her, but it turned out not to be about her.

'It's about the young man – Antoine, if I got the name correctly.'

'Yes, Antoine. Has he run away again?'

'That's right. Apparently, you asked yesterday for an inspector to tail him. The young man went straight home to Faubourg Saint-Martin, almost on the corner of Rue Louis-Blanc. The inspector Judel had assigned to the job questioned the concierge. The boy lives with his mother, who's a cleaning lady, on the seventh floor of the building.

They have two attic rooms. There's no lift. I'm telling you all this just as Judel told it to me. Apparently, the building is one of those awful tenements where fifty or sixty families are packed in and the kids have to play on the stairs.'

'Go on.'

'That's pretty much it. According to the concierge, the young man's mother is a brave, deserving woman. Her husband died in a sanatorium. She's had TB as well and claims she's cured, but the concierge doubts it. Getting back to the inspector, he phoned Judel to ask for instructions. Judel didn't want to take any risks and ordered him to keep an eye on the building. He stayed outside until about midnight, after which he went in with the last tenants and spent the night on the stairs.

'This morning, just before eight, the concierge pointed out to him a thin woman who was walking past the lodge and told him it was Antoine's mother. The inspector had no reason to stop her or follow her. It was only half an hour later, when he had nothing better to do, that he was curious enough to go up to the seventh floor.

'It struck him as odd that the boy hadn't also come downstairs to go to work. He stuck his ear to the door, didn't hear anything and knocked. Eventually, noticing that the lock was a very simple one, he tried his skeleton key.

'He saw a bed in the first room, which is also the kitchen, the mother's bed, and in the next room, another bed, unmade. But there was nobody there, and the skylight was open.

'Judel's annoyed that he didn't think of that and didn't

give orders accordingly. It's obvious that in the course of the night the boy got out through the skylight and walked over the roofs looking for another open skylight. He probably got out through a building in Rue Louis-Blanc.'

'Are they sure he isn't still in the building?'

'They're questioning the tenants right now.'

Maigret could imagine Judge Coméliau's ironic smile on hearing this news.

'Has Lapointe called me?'

'Not yet.'

'Has anybody shown up at the Forensic Institute to identify the body?'

'Just the usual customers.'

There were about a dozen of them, especially women of a certain age, who rush to identify every unidentified body that is found.

'Has Dr Paul phoned?'

'I've just put his report on your desk.'

'If Lapointe calls, tell him to come back here and wait for me. I'm not going far.'

He headed on foot for the Ile Saint-Louis, walked around the outside of Notre-Dame, crossed the iron foot-bridge and soon found himself in the narrow, populous Rue Saint-Louis-en-l'Ile. It was the time of day when the housewives were doing their shopping, and it wasn't easy to make your way through them and the little barrows. Maigret found the grocery above which, according to Madame Calas, her daughter, whose name was Lucette, had a room. He walked down the side alley next to the shop until he came to a yard with uneven cobbles and a lime tree in the middle, giving it the air of a provincial school playground or the courtyard of a presbytery.

'Are you looking for someone?' a woman's voice cried through a ground-floor window.

'Mademoiselle Calas.'

'Third floor on the left, but she isn't at home.'

'Do you know when she'll be back?'

'She doesn't usually come back for lunch. We don't often see her before half past six. If it's urgent, you'll find her at the hospital.'

The Hôtel-Dieu, where Lucette Calas worked, wasn't far. All the same, it was a complicated business getting to Professor Lavaud's department because it was the busiest time of the day, and men and women in white uniforms, male nurses pushing stretchers and patients with uncertain steps kept up a steady flow in the corridors, going through doors that led God alone knew where.

'Mademoiselle Calas, please?'

They barely looked at him.

'Don't know her. Is she a patient?'

Or else they would point him to the end of a corridor:

'Through there.'

He was sent in three or four different directions until all at once, as if reaching a safe haven, he came to a quiet corridor where a young woman was sitting at a small table.

'Mademoiselle Calas?'

'Is it personal? How did you get in?'

He must have wandered into an area that wasn't accessible to ordinary mortals. He gave his name and even showed his badge, feeling that here his prestige counted for little.

'I'll go and see if she can be disturbed. I think she might be in the operating theatre.'

He was left alone for a good ten minutes and didn't dare smoke. When the young woman returned, she was followed by a fairly tall nurse with a calm, serene face.

'Is it you who wants to speak to me?'

'Detective Chief Inspector Maigret, Police Judiciaire.'

Because of the bright, clean atmosphere of the hospital, the white uniform, the nurse's cap, the contrast was all the more striking with the bistro on Quai de Valmy.

Lucette Calas seemed untroubled, but looked at him in surprise, like someone who doesn't understand.

'It is me you want to see?'

'If your parents live on Quai de Valmy, yes.'

It was very brief, but Maigret was certain he saw something like a harder gleam in her eyes.

'Yes. But I—'

'I just want to ask you a few questions.'

'The professor's going to need me very soon. He's doing his rounds right now and—'

'It'll only take a few minutes.'

She resigned herself, looked around and spotted a half-open door.

'We can go in here.'

There were two chairs, an adjustable bed and instruments that must have been surgical but which Maigret didn't know.

'When was the last time you went to visit your parents?'

He noticed a shudder at the word 'parents' and thought he knew the reason.

'I go as seldom as possible.'

'Why?'

'Have you seen them?'

'I've seen your mother.'

She said nothing, as if it was self-explanatory.

'Do you resent them?'

'I can hardly resent them, unless it's for giving birth to me.'

'Did you go there last Friday?'

'I wasn't even in Paris. It was my day off, and I was in the country with friends.'

'So you don't know why your father's away?'

'Aren't you going to tell me why you're asking me these questions? You come here and talk to me about people who are officially my parents but with whom I've long felt a stranger. Why? Has something happened to them?'

She lit a cigarette and as she did so said:

'You can smoke here. At least at this time of day.'

But he didn't take advantage of the offer to get out his pipe.

'Would it surprise you if something had happened to one of them?'

She looked straight at him.

'No,' she said.

'What do you think might have happened, for example?'

'Calas might have beaten my mother so badly that she's really hurt.'

She hadn't said 'my father', but 'Calas'.

'Does he often beat her?'

'I don't know about now. In the old days, it was almost daily.'

'Didn't your mother protest?'

'She'd bow her head and let him do it. Maybe she likes it, I don't know.'

'What else might have happened?'

'She might have decided to put poison in his soup.'

'Does she hate him?'

'All I know is that she's lived with him for twenty-four years and never tried to run away.'

'Do you think she's unhappy?'

'You know something, inspector? I try not to think about it at all. When I was a child, my one dream was to leave. And as soon as I could, I did.'

'You were fifteen, I know.'

'Who told you?'

'Your mother.'

'So he hasn't killed her.'

She seemed to think about this, then lifted her head.

'Is it him?'

'What do you mean?'

'Has she poisoned him?'

'It's not very likely. In fact, it's by no means certain anything has happened to him at all. Your mother claims he left on Friday afternoon for the Poitiers area, which is where he apparently buys his white wine.'

'That's right. He was already making those trips when I was around.'

'At the same time, a body that might be his has been fished out of the Canal Saint-Martin.'

'Has it been identified?'

'Not yet. What makes identification particularly difficult is that we haven't found the head.'

Perhaps because she worked in a hospital, this didn't even make her retch.

'What do you think happened to him?' she asked.

'I don't know. I'm trying to find out. There seem to be quite a few men in your mother's life. I'm sorry to talk to you about that.'

'So what else is new?'

'Did your father once, when he was a child or an adolescent, get shot in the stomach with a shotgun?'

She looked surprised. 'I never heard about that.'

'Of course, you never saw any scars?'

'Not if they're on his stomach,' she said with a slight smile.

'When was the last time you went to Quai de Valmy?'

'Let me see . . . It must have been about a month ago.'

'Did you go on a visit, the way people usually visit their parents?'

'Not exactly.'

'Was Calas there?'

'I make sure I go when he isn't there.'

'In the afternoon?'

'Yes. He usually plays billiards somewhere near Gare de l'Est.'

'There wasn't a man with your mother?'

'Not that day.'

'Did you have a particular reason to visit her?'

'No.'

'What did you talk about?'

'I don't remember. This and that.'

'Did you talk about Calas?'

'I doubt it.'

'You didn't by any chance go to see your mother to ask for money?'

'You're barking up the wrong tree, inspector. Rightly or wrongly, I have my pride. There have been times when I was short of money, I've even been hungry, but I've never knocked at their door and begged for help. And I certainly wouldn't do it now that I'm earning a decent living.'

'Can you remember anything that was said during your last conversation with your mother?'

'Nothing in particular.'

'Among the men you sometimes saw there, was there an aggressive young man who rides a delivery tricycle?'

She shook her head.

'Or a middle-aged man with red hair?'

This time, she stopped to think.

'Does he have a pockmarked face?' she asked.

'I don't know.'

'If he does, that's Monsieur Dieudonné.'

'Who's Monsieur Dieudonné?'

'I don't really know much more than that. He's a friend of my mother's. He's been a customer there for years.'

'An afternoon customer?'

She knew what he meant. 'Well, it was always in the afternoon that I saw him. But it might not be what you think. I really can't say. He struck me as a quiet man, the kind you can imagine in the evening by the fire in his slippers. Actually, that's almost always where I saw him, sitting by the stove, opposite my mother. They looked as if they'd known each other for a long time, as if they didn't need to put themselves out for each other any more. You know what I mean? You could have taken them for an old couple.'

'Do you have any idea where he lives?'

'Once when he stood up to go, I heard him say, in a soft voice I'd recognize, "I have to get back to work," so I assume he works locally, but I don't know what he does. He doesn't dress like a factory worker. I suspect he's some kind of clerk.'

They heard a bell in the corridor, and Lucette automatically sprang to her feet.

'That's for me,' she said. 'You'll have to excuse me.'

'It's possible I may need to see you again at home.'

'I'm only there in the evenings. Don't come too late, I go to bed early.'

He saw her shake her head as she walked along the corridor, like someone who isn't yet accustomed to a new thought.

'I beg your pardon, mademoiselle. How do I get to the exit?'

He seemed so lost that the girl sitting at the desk smiled and led him down the corridor to a staircase.

'From here on, it's plain sailing. When you get downstairs, turn left, then left again.'

'Thank you.'

He didn't dare ask her what she thought of Lucette

Calas. As for what he thought of her himself, he would have found it hard to say.

He stopped for a moment for a white wine, opposite the Palais de Justice. By the time he got back to headquarters, Lapointe had arrived and was waiting for him.

'So, what about the nuns?'

'They were as nice as could be. I was afraid I'd feel uncomfortable, but they were so kind that—'

'Tell me about the scars.'

Lapointe wasn't as delighted with the outcome.

'First of all, the doctor who performed the operation died three years ago, as Madame Calas said. The nun who runs the office found the file. There's no mention of scars, which is quite normal, but, on the other hand, I did learn that Calas had a stomach ulcer.'

'Did they operate on it?'

'No. Before an operation, they apparently do a complete examination and record the results.'

'Was there any mention of distinguishing marks?'

'Nothing like that. The nun was kind enough to ask the other nuns who might have been present at the operation. None of them remembers Calas very clearly. Just one of them thinks she remembers that before he was put to sleep he asked to be allowed time to say a prayer.'

'Was he a practising Catholic?'

'No. He was afraid. That's the kind of detail the nuns don't forget. They didn't notice any scars.'

So no progress had been made, and they were still dealing with a headless body it was impossible to identify with any degree of certainty.

'What do we do?' Lapointe asked in a low voice, seeing how grouchy Maigret was.

Wasn't Judge Coméliau right? If the dead man in the Canal Saint-Martin was Omer Calas, then there was a good chance that if they subjected his wife to a tough interrogation they would get some valuable information out of her. A sit-down with Antoine the delivery boy, when they could get their hands on him, would almost certainly pay dividends, too.

'Come.'

'Shall I take the car?'

'Yes.'

'Where are we going?'

'To the canal.'

In the meantime, he would ask the inspectors of the tenth arrondissement to look locally for a red-headed man with a pockmarked face who answered to the name Dieudonné.

The car weaved its way between the buses and lorries and had just reached Boulevard Richard-Lenoir, not far from Maigret's apartment, when the inspector grunted:

'Go via Gare de l'Est.'

Lapointe looked at him as if he didn't understand.

'It may not lead to anything, but I prefer to check. We're told that Calas left on Friday afternoon, taking his suitcase with him. Let's say he came back on Saturday. If it was him they killed and cut into pieces, they would have had to get rid of that suitcase. I'm convinced it's not in the house any more, and nor are the clothes he's supposed to have taken with him on his trip.'

Lapointe was nodding as he followed Maigret's argument.

'We haven't found any suitcase in the canal, or any clothes, even though the corpse was undressed before being dismembered.'

'And we haven't found the head!' Lapointe added.

There was nothing original about Maigret's hypothesis. It was just a matter of routine. Six times out of ten, when guilty parties want to dispose of compromising objects, they simply deposit them in a station left luggage office.

Gare de l'Est, as it happened, was not far from Quai de Valmy. Lapointe finally managed to park the car and followed Maigret into the concourse.

'Were you on duty on Friday afternoon?' he asked the employee at the left luggage office.

'Only until six.'

'Was a lot of luggage deposited?'

'No more than any other day.'

'Among the items deposited on Friday, are there any that haven't yet been collected?'

The employee turned towards the racks on which stood suitcases and packages of all kinds.

'Two!' he replied.

'Both belonging to the same person?'

'No. The numbers aren't consecutive. And the crate covered in canvas was left by a fat woman who I remember, because I noticed that she smelled of cheese.'

'Is there cheese in it?'

'I have no idea. Actually, no, it doesn't smell any more. So maybe it really was the woman who smelled.'

'And the second item?'

'It's a brown suitcase.'

He pointed to a cheap suitcase that had clearly been much used.

'Does it have a name or address on it?'

'No.'

'Do you remember the person who brought it?'

'I may be wrong, but I'd swear it was a young man from the country.'

'Why from the country?'

'The way he looked.'

'Because he had a ruddy face?'

'Maybe.'

'How was he dressed?'

'I think he had a leather jacket and a cap.'

Maigret and Lapointe looked at each other, both thinking of Antoine Cristin.

'What time would that have been?'

'About five. Yes. Just after five, because the express from Strasbourg had just pulled in.'

'If anyone comes to collect the suitcase, can you telephone the police station on Quai de Jemmapes right away?'

'What if the guy takes fright and runs away?'

'Even if he does, we'll be here in a few minutes.'

There was only one way to identify the suitcase, and that was to go and see Madame Calas and show it to her. She watched indifferently as the two men entered the bistro and walked to the counter to serve them.

'We won't be drinking anything right now,' Maigret said. 'We've come to see you because we want you to identify an object that's not far from here. My inspector will go with you.'

'Do I have to shut up shop?'

'There's no need, you'll be back in a few minutes. I'll stay here.'

She didn't put on a hat, merely swapped her slippers for shoes.

'Are you going to serve the customers?'

'I probably won't need to.'

When the car drove off, with Lapointe at the wheel and Madame Calas beside him, Maigret stood for a moment in the doorway, a curious smile on his lips. It was the first time in his career that he had been alone in a bistro as if he were the owner, and the idea amused him so much that he slipped behind the counter.

5. The Bottle of Ink

The sunbeams formed patterns in the same places as on the morning of the previous day, including an animal-shaped one on the rounded corner of the tin counter, and another on a chromo depicting a woman in a red dress holding out a glass of foamy beer.

As Maigret had already felt the day before, this little bistro, like many such places in Paris, had something of the atmosphere of one of those country inns that are empty for most of the week but suddenly fill up on market days.

He might have been tempted to pour himself a drink, but it was a childish desire that embarrassed him. Hands in his pockets, pipe between his teeth, he walked to the door at the back.

He hadn't yet seen what was behind that door, through which Madame Calas often disappeared. As he had expected, he found a kitchen which was somewhat untidy, but less dirty than he had imagined. On a brown-painted wooden sideboard immediately to the left of the door stood an already started bottle of cognac. So it wasn't wine that Madame Calas drank throughout the day, but brandy. There was no glass beside it, which meant she was probably in the habit of drinking it straight from the bottle.

A window looked out on the yard, as well as a glass door which wasn't locked and which he now opened. There were a line of empty casks in a corner, a heap of straw cases that been used to wrap bottles, buckets with holes in them, rusty iron hoops. The illusion of being a long way from Paris was so strong that he wouldn't have been surprised to see a pile of manure and some chickens.

Beyond the yard was a blind alley with windowless walls that probably led to a sidestreet.

Mechanically, he looked up at the windows on the first floor of the bistro. They clearly hadn't been washed for a long time, and the curtains hanging at them were faded. He might have been wrong, but he had the feeling that something had moved behind those windows. He was sure he had just seen the cat lying by the stove.

Unhurriedly, he went back into the kitchen and began climbing the spiral staircase that led upstairs. The steps creaked. Even the vague smell of mildew reminded him of little village inns where he had sometimes spent the night.

Two doors led off the landing. He opened one and found himself in what must be the Calas couple's bedroom. It looked out on the quayside. The walnut double bed hadn't been made that morning and the sheets were quite clean. The furniture was the kind he would have found in any apartment of this kind, old furniture passed down from father to son, heavy and polished smooth by time.

In the wardrobe, a man's clothes were hanging. Between the windows was an armchair covered in dark-red rep and beside it an old-fashioned radio. In the middle of the room, finally, was a round table covered in a cloth of an indefinable colour, flanked by two mahogany chairs.

He wondered what it was that had struck him as soon as he came in and had to look around the room several times before his gaze came to rest again on the tablecloth. A new-looking bottle of ink stood on it, along with a penholder and one of those promotional blotting pads placed at the disposal of customers in bistros.

He opened it, without expecting to make a discovery, and indeed he didn't make one, finding in it only three sheets of white paper. At the same time he pricked up his ears, thinking he heard a creaking. It hadn't come from the toilet, which led directly off the bedroom. Going back to the landing, he opened the second door and discovered another room, as big as the previous one, which served as a store room and was cluttered with furniture in poor condition, old magazines, glassware and all manner of miscellaneous objects.

'Is there anybody here?' he asked in a loud voice, almost certain he wasn't alone in the room.

He stood there for a moment, motionless, then silently reached out his arm to a closet and abruptly opened it.

'Don't do anything stupid this time,' he said.

He wasn't too surprised to recognize Antoine, who sat huddled at the back of the closet like a hunted animal.

'I thought we'd find you soon enough. Get out of there!'

'Are you arresting me?'

The young man was looking in terror at the handcuffs that Maigret had taken from his pocket.

'I don't know yet what I'm going to do with you, but I

have no intention of letting you vanish into thin air again. Hold out your wrists.'

'You have no right. I haven't done anything.'

'Hold out your wrists!'

He guessed that the boy was hesitating over whether or not to chance his luck and try to get away. Moving forwards, he used his whole bulk to pin him to the wall. After the boy had struggled a little, kicking him in the legs, he managed to close the handcuffs.

'Now follow me!'

'What did my mother say?'

'I have no idea what your mother's going to say about this, but we have a certain number of questions to ask you.'

'I won't answer them.'

'Come anyway.'

He made him go in front. They walked through the kitchen. When Antoine entered the bar, he was struck by the emptiness and the silence.

'Where is she?'

'Madame Calas? Don't worry. She'll be back.'

'Have you arrested her?'

'Sit down in that corner and don't move.'

'I'll move if I want to!'

He had seen so many young people that age, in more or less similar situations, that he could have predicted everything Antoine said, the way he reacted to everything.

Because of Judge Coméliau, Maigret wasn't sorry to have got his hands on Antoine, but nor was he expecting the boy to clear things up for him.

Someone opened the street door, a middle-aged man

who was surprised to find Maigret standing there in the middle of the bistro, with no sign of Madame Calas.

'Isn't the lady here?'

'She'll be back soon.'

Did the man see the handcuffs? Did he realize that Maigret was a policeman? Was that why he didn't come any closer? He touched his cap and hurried out, stammering something like:

'I'll be back.'

He couldn't have got to the corner of the street before the black car stopped outside the door and Lapointe got out first, opened the car door for Madame Calas and took a brown suitcase out of the car.

Madame Calas saw Antoine immediately, frowned and turned anxiously to Maigret.

'Didn't you know he was in your house?'

'Don't answer!' the young man said to her. 'He has no right to arrest me. I haven't done anything. I challenge him to prove I've done anything wrong.'

Without further delay, Maigret turned to Lapointe.

'Is this the suitcase?'

'She wasn't too sure at first, then she said yes, then she said she couldn't be certain without opening it.'

'Have you opened it?'

'I wanted you to be present. I gave the man at the station a temporary receipt. He insists we send him an official requisition application as soon as possible.'

'Ask Coméliau for one. Is the man still there?'

'I suppose so. He didn't look as if he was about to go off duty.'

'Phone him. Ask him if someone can replace him for a quarter of an hour. It shouldn't be impossible. Tell him to get in a taxi and come here.'

'Got it,' Lapointe said, looking at Antoine.

Was the man from the left luggage office going to recognize him? If he did, everything would get even easier.

'Phone Moers. I'd like him to come, too, and carry out a proper search, along with photographers.'

'Right, chief.'

Madame Calas, who was standing there in the middle of the room, as if paying a visit, now also asked, as Antoine had already done:

'Are you arresting me?'

She seemed disconcerted when Maigret simply replied:

'Why?'

'Can I come and go as I please?'

'In the house, yes.'

He knew what she wanted, and indeed, she walked straight to the kitchen and disappeared into the corner where the bottle of cognac was. To cover her tracks, she moved some dishes and swapped her shoes, which she wasn't used to and probably hurt her feet, for her felt slippers.

When she returned, she had regained her composure. She went behind the counter.

'Can I get you a drink?'

'A white wine, yes. And one for the inspector. Maybe Antoine would like a glass of beer?'

He was behaving like a man who has plenty of time. It might even have been supposed that he had no idea what he was going to do from one moment to the next. Having sipped at his wine, he walked to the door and locked it.

'Do you have the key to the suitcase?'

'No.'

'Do you know where it is?'

'Probably in "his" pocket.'

In Calas' pocket, since he was supposed to have left the house with his suitcase.

'I need some kind of tool. Do you have any pliers?'

It took her a while to lay her hands on a pair of pliers. Maigret placed the suitcase on one of the tables and waited for Lapointe to finish making his telephone calls before starting to force the not very strong lock.

'I ordered a white wine for you.'

'Thank you, chief.'

The metal twisted and finally snapped, and Maigret lifted the lid. Madame Calas had remained on the other side of the counter. Although she was looking in their direction, she didn't appear especially interested.

The suitcase contained a grey suit of rather thin fabric, a pair of almost new shoes, some shirts, some socks, a razor, a comb and a toothbrush as well as a bar of soap wrapped in paper.

'Is this your husband's?'

'I suppose so.'

'Aren't you sure?'

'He does own a suit like that.'

'Isn't it upstairs any more?'

'I haven't looked.'

She wasn't helping them, nor was she trying to allay

suspicion. Since the day before, she had been answering questions in as few words and with as few details as possible, although without ever becoming as aggressive as Antoine, for instance.

Antoine was so scared, he kept getting on his high horse, whereas Madame Calas didn't seem to have anything to fear. The comings and goings of the police officers, the discoveries they might make, were a matter of indifference to her.

'Do you notice anything?' Maigret said to Lapointe as he looked through the suitcase.

'That everything has been stuffed in just anyhow?'

'Yes. That's how men pack most of the time. There's something odder than that. Calas was supposedly going on a journey. He took a spare suit with him, as well as shoes and underwear. In theory, he would have packed upstairs in the bedroom.'

Two men in plasterers' overalls shook the door, stuck their faces to the window, seemed to be yelling something that couldn't be heard and walked off.

'Can you tell me why, in that situation, he would have taken dirty linen with him?'

One of the two shirts, indeed, had been worn, as had a pair of pants and a pair of socks.

'You think he wasn't the one who put these things in the case?'

'It might have been him. It probably was. But not when he was leaving for his trip. When he packed his bag, he was on the point of coming home.'

'I see.'

'Did you hear that, Madame Calas?'

She nodded.

'Do you still claim that your husband left on Friday afternoon and took this case with him?'

'I have nothing to change in what I said.'

'Are you sure he wasn't here on Thursday? And that it wasn't Friday that he *came home*?'

She merely shook her head.

'Whatever I say, you'll believe what you want to believe.'

A taxi stopped outside. Maigret went to open the door. The employee from the left luggage office got out of the cab.

'Keep the taxi. I'll only need you for a moment.'

Maigret let him in. For a moment or two, the man stood there wondering what they wanted of him, looking around to get his bearings. His gaze came to rest on Antoine, who was still sitting in the corner of the banquette.

He turned to Maigret and opened his mouth. Then he examined the boy again.

During all this time, which seemed long, Antoine looked him in the eyes with a defiant air.

'I think . . .' the man began, scratching the back of his neck.

He was honest and was struggling with his conscience.

'I have to say, seeing him like this, I'd say it's him.'

'You're lying!' the boy cried angrily.

'It might be easier if he was standing.'

'Stand up.'

'No.'

'Stand up!'

Madame Calas' voice, behind Maigret's back, said:

'Stand up, Antoine.'

'Like this,' the man murmured after a moment's thought, 'I'm a bit surer. Doesn't he have a leather jacket?'

'Have a look upstairs, in the room at the back,' Maigret said to Lapointe.

They waited in silence. The man glanced towards the counter, and Maigret understood that he was thirsty.

'A glass of white wine?' he asked.

'I wouldn't say no.'

Lapointe returned with the jacket that Antoine had been wearing the day before.

'Put it on.'

The young man looked at Madame Calas to ask her advice. Reluctantly, he resigned himself, once the handcuffs had been removed.

'Don't you see how he's trying to get in with the coppers? They're all the same. You just have to say the word "police" and they start shaking. Well, now, are you still going to claim you've seen me before?'

'I think so.'

'You're lying.'

The man turned again to Maigret and said in a calm voice that nevertheless quivered with emotion:

'I assume my statement's important? I wouldn't like to harm anyone for nothing. This young man looks like the one who came to the station on Sunday and deposited the suitcase. Since I had no idea anybody was going to ask me about him, I didn't look at him all that closely. Maybe, if I saw him in the same place, in the same lighting . . .'

'We'll bring him to the station today or tomorrow,' Maigret decided. 'I'm very grateful to you. Cheers!'

He walked him to the door and closed it behind him. There was a kind of indefinable slackness in Maigret's attitude that rather intrigued Lapointe, who couldn't have said when it had started. Maybe it dated from right at the beginning of the investigation, from as soon as they had got to Quai de Valmy the day before, or as soon as they had entered the Calas bistro.

Maigret was acting as he usually did, was doing what he had to do. But wasn't he doing it with a lack of conviction that his inspectors had seldom seen in him? It was hard to define. He seemed to be acting rather reluctantly. The material clues barely interested him, and he appeared to be pondering thoughts that he wasn't conveying to anyone.

It was especially noticeable here, in this bistro, and even more so whenever he addressed Madame Calas or watched her out of the corner of his eye.

It was as if the victim didn't count, as if the dismembered body meant nothing to him. He had barely bothered with Antoine and he had to make an effort to think of certain professional duties.

'Call Coméliau. I'd prefer it to be you. Tell him in a few words what's happened. It's probably best if he signs a committal order for the boy. He'll do it anyway.'

'What about her?' Lapointe asked, indicating Madame Calas.

'I'd rather not.'

'What if he insists?'

'He'll do what he wants. He's in charge.'

He didn't take the precaution of speaking in a low voice, and the other two were listening.

'You ought to have a bite to eat,' he advised Madame Calas. 'They may be taking you away soon.'

'For a long time?'

'For as long as the magistrate sees fit to keep you at his disposal.'

'Will I spend the night in prison?'

'In the cells at headquarters first, probably.'

'What about me?' Antoine asked.

'You, too,' Maigret replied, adding: 'Not in the same cell!'

'Are you hungry?' Madame Calas asked Antoine.

'No.'

She nevertheless headed for the kitchen, but only to knock back a swig of brandy. When she returned, she asked:

'Who'll mind the store while I'm away?'

'Nobody. Don't worry. We'll keep an eye on it.'

He couldn't stop looking at her, still in the same way, as if for the first time he was dealing with somebody he didn't understand.

He had met some clever women in his career, and some had stood up to him for a long time. But he'd always known from the start that he would eventually gain the upper hand. It was a matter of time, patience and determination.

With Madame Calas, it wasn't the same. He couldn't put her in any category. If someone had told him that she had murdered her husband in cold blood and cut him into pieces on the kitchen table, he wouldn't have objected. But nor would he have objected if someone had asserted that she had no idea what had happened to her husband.

There she was, in front of him, in the flesh, thin and faded in her dark dress, which hung on her body like an old curtain hanging at a window. She was quite real, with the gleam of an intense inner life in her dark eyes, and yet there was something immaterial, something elusive about her.

Did she know she produced that impression? You might have thought so from the calm, perhaps ironic way in which she, too, looked at Maigret.

That was the source of the unease Lapointe had felt earlier. This was less a police investigation to discover a culprit than a personal matter between Maigret and this woman.

Whatever didn't relate directly to her was of lesser interest to Maigret. Lapointe was to have proof of that a moment later, when he came out of the phone booth.

'What did he say?' Maigret asked, referring to Coméliau.

'He'll sign an order and have it brought to your office.'

'Does he want to see him?'

'He assumes you'll want to question him first.'

'What about her?'

'He'll sign a second order. You can do what you want with it, but in my opinion . . .'

'I understand.'

Coméliau was expecting Maigret to go back to his office, summon Antoine and Madame Calas in turn and question them for hours until they spilled the beans.

The head still hadn't been found. There was no positive

proof that the man whose remains had been fished out of the Canal Saint-Martin was Omer Calas. At least now, because of the suitcase, there was a strong presumption of guilt, and many interrogations, started with fewer advantages than this one, had ended after a few hours in a complete confession.

Not only was that Judge Coméliau's thought, it was also Lapointe's, and he could barely conceal his surprise when Maigret said:

'Take him to headquarters. Go with him to my office and question him. Don't forget to bring him up something to eat and drink.'

'Are you staying here?'

'I'll wait for Moers and the photographers.'

Embarrassed, Lapointe motioned to the young man to stand up. Before leaving, Antoine yelled at Maigret:

'I warn you, you'll pay for this.'

At almost the same moment, the viscount, who had been prowling the various offices of the Police Judiciaire as he did every morning, was continuing his rounds in the examining magistrates' corridor.

'Nothing new, Monsieur Coméliau? Haven't they found the head yet?'

'Not yet. But we have an almost positive identification.'

'Who is he?'

For ten minutes, Coméliau gladly answered questions, not sorry that for once it was he and not Maigret who had the attention of the press.

'Is the inspector over there?'

'I imagine so.'

And so the search of the Calas residence and the arrest of a young man, known so far only by his initials, were announced two hours later in the afternoon newspapers, then on the five o'clock bulletin on the radio.

Alone now with Madame Calas, Maigret had gone to fetch a drink from the counter and had carried it over to a table and sat down. For her part, she hadn't moved, remaining behind the bar in the classic pose of the bistro owner's wife.

They heard the factory sirens announcing midday. In less than ten minutes, more than thirty people came and stuck their noses against the closed door. Some, seeing Madame Calas through the window, gesticulated as if trying to argue with her.

'I saw your daughter,' Maigret said suddenly, breaking the silence.

She looked at him without saying a word.

'She confirmed that she came to visit you about a month ago. I wonder what the two of you talked about.'

It wasn't a question, and she didn't see fit to answer.

'I got the impression she's a well-balanced person, who's been clever enough to do well for herself. I don't know why, but it crossed my mind that she's in love with her boss and may even be his mistress.'

She still didn't react. Did any of this interest her? Did she have any feelings for her daughter?

'It can't have been easy for her at first. It's hard for a girl of fifteen to get by alone in a city like Paris.'

She looked at him with eyes that seemed to see through him.

'What is it you want?' she asked in a weary voice.

Yes, what was it he wanted? Wasn't Coméliau right? Shouldn't he be grilling Antoine right now? And wouldn't a few days in the cells at headquarters change Madame Calas' attitude?

'I wonder why you married Calas and why, later, you didn't leave him.'

It wasn't a smile that came to her lips but an expression that might pass for mockery – or pity.

'You did it deliberately, didn't you?' Maigret continued without clarifying what he meant.

He had to get there in the end. There were moments, like now, when it seemed to him that it would only take a slight effort, not only for him to understand everything, but for that invisible wall between them to disappear.

Find the word that had to be said, and then she would be simply human towards him.

'Was the other man here on Friday afternoon?'

This time he obtained a result: she gave a start.

'What other man?' she finally asked reluctantly.

'Your lover. The real one.'

She would have liked to appear indifferent and not ask any questions, but she finally yielded.

'Who?'

'A middle-aged man with red hair and a pockmarked face, whose first name is Dieudonné.'

She had completely withdrawn back into her shell. There was nothing more to read in her features. At that moment, a car drew up outside, and Moers got out, with three men and their equipment.

Once more, Maigret went and opened the door. No, he hadn't succeeded. But he didn't think he had completely wasted the time he had just spent alone with her.

'What do you want us to look at, chief?'

'Everything. The kitchen first, then the two rooms and the toilet on the first floor. There's also the courtyard and, last but not least, the cellar which is probably under this trapdoor.'

'Do you think this is where the man was killed and dismembered?'

'It's possible.'

'What about this suitcase?'

'Examine it, as well as its contents.'

'That could take all afternoon. Are you staying?'

'I don't think so, but I'll probably drop by later.'

He went into the booth, called Judel at the police station opposite and gave him instructions for the house to remain under surveillance.

'You'd do better to come with me,' he announced to Madame Calas.

'Shall I take some clothes and toiletries?'

'That might be wise.'

On her way through the kitchen, she stopped for a long swig. They then heard her walking about in the bedroom on the first floor.

'Aren't you afraid of leaving her on her own, chief?'

Maigret shrugged. If there were traces to wipe out, compromising objects to get rid of, that must have been taken care of a long time ago.

He was surprised, however, that she was away for so

long. They could still hear her moving about, and there were sounds of water running and drawers being opened and closed.

In the kitchen, she stopped again. She was probably telling herself that this was the last brandy she would have a chance to drink in a while.

When she finally appeared, the three men looked at her with the same surprise, a surprise that, in Maigret, was mixed with a touch of admiration.

In less than twenty minutes, she had undergone an almost complete transformation. She was now wearing a black dress and coat that made her look very elegant. With her hair done and a nice hat on, it was as if the features of her face themselves had become firmer, her gait more distinct, her bearing resolute, almost proud.

Had she been expecting the effect she produced? Was there an element of flirtatiousness? She didn't smile, didn't seem amused at their surprise, merely made sure she had what she needed in her bag, put on her gloves and said:

'I'm ready.'

She gave off an unexpected smell of eau de Cologne and cognac. She had powdered her face and painted her lips.

'Aren't you taking a case?'

She said no, as if defiantly. Taking a change of clothes and underwear would be tantamount to admitting guilt – or at least to admitting that there might be good reasons to detain her.

'See you later!' Maigret said to Moers and his colleagues.

'Are you taking the car?'

'No. I'll find a taxi.'

It made a curious impression on him to find himself with her on the pavement and to walk in step with her in the sunshine.

'I suppose we have more chance of finding a taxi if we walk down to Rue des Récollets?'

'I suppose so.'

'I'd like to ask you a question.'

'You haven't been shy so far.'

'How long is it since you last dressed like that?'

She took the trouble to think this over.

'At least four years,' she said at last. 'Why do you ask?'

'No reason.'

What was the point of telling her, since she knew as well as he did? Just in time, he raised his arm to stop a passing taxi. He opened the door for his companion and let her get in first.

6. The Threads of String

To tell the truth, he didn't yet know what he was going to do with her. It was quite likely that with another examining magistrate he wouldn't have acted as he had done so far and would have taken more risks. With Coméliau, that was dangerous. Not only was the magistrate finicky, anxious to observe the formalities, worried about public opinion and the reaction of the government, but he had always viewed Maigret's methods with suspicion, finding them unorthodox. Several times in the past, the two men had clashed openly.

Maigret knew that the magistrate had his eye on him, ready to make him bear responsibility for the slightest mistake, the slightest imprudent move.

He would much have preferred to leave Madame Calas at home on Quai de Valmy until he'd built up a clearer idea of her character and the role she might have played. He would have put one or two men to keep watch on the bistro. But had Judel's officer stopped young Antoine escaping from the building on Faubourg Saint-Martin? Antoine was nothing but a boy, with not much more intelligence than a child of thirteen. Madame Calas was quite another matter. As they passed the newsstands, he could see that the papers were already announcing the search of the bistro. In any case, the name Calas was in all the headlines.

He imagined how it would be if, next day for example, the morning newspapers announced 'Madame Calas has disappeared', and he had to go in and see the magistrate.

Without turning his head to her, he was watching her out of the corner of his eye. She didn't seem to notice. She was holding herself very upright on her seat, not without dignity, and there was curiosity in the way she looked out at the city.

She hadn't dressed up for at least four years, she had admitted earlier. She hadn't said in what circumstances, on what occasion, she had last worn her black dress. Had it been even longer since she had last gone to the centre of town and seen the crush of people on the boulevards?

Since he couldn't do exactly what he wanted, because of Coméliau, he was forced to go about it differently.

As they neared Quai des Orfèvres, he opened his mouth for the first time.

'I don't suppose you have anything to say?'

She looked at him with a hint of surprise.

'What about?'

'About your husband.'

She shrugged imperceptibly.

'I didn't kill Calas,' she said.

She called him by his surname, the way the wives of some peasants and shopkeepers are in the habit of calling their husbands. That struck Maigret, as if, coming from her, it didn't sound natural.

'Shall I drive into the courtyard?' the driver asked, opening his window.

'If you like.'

The viscount was there, at the foot of the grand staircase, with two other journalists and some photographers. They'd had wind of what was happening, and it was pointless trying to hide the prisoner from them.

'One moment, detective chief inspector . . .'

Did she think it was Maigret who had asked for them to come? She walked past them, very stiffly, while they took photographs and followed her up the stairs. They must have photographed young Antoine, too.

Even upstairs, in the corridor, Maigret still hesitated. He opened the door to the inspectors' office. Lucas wasn't there. He spoke to Janvier instead.

'Can you take her into an empty office for a few minutes and stay with her?'

She had heard. There was still a silent reproach in the gaze she brought to bear on Maigret. Or was it more disappointment than reproach?

He walked out without adding anything and went into his own office, where Lapointe, who had taken off his jacket, was sitting in his place. Opposite the window, Antoine was sitting upright on his chair. He looked very red, as if he was too hot.

Between them, on a tray that had been brought up from the Brasserie Dauphine, could be seen the remains of sandwiches and two glasses with dregs of beer at the bottom.

As Maigret's eyes came to rest on the tray, then on him, Antoine seemed upset at having yielded to his appetite, presumably having previously vowed to 'punish' them by refusing all food. They were used to that kind of attitude here, and Maigret couldn't help smiling.

'How's it going?' he asked Lapointe.

With his eyes, Lapointe made it clear that he had obtained nothing so far.

'Carry on, boys!'

He walked upstairs to see Coméliau and found him in his office, ready to go to lunch.

'Have you arrested both of them?'

'The young man's in my office, Lapointe is questioning him.'

'Has he talked?'

'Even if he knows something, he won't say anything until we wave the evidence right under his nose.'

'Is he bright?'

'That's just it, he isn't. You usually end up by getting the better of someone intelligent, if only by demonstrating that his answers don't stand up. An idiot simply denies everything, in spite of the evidence.'

'What about the woman?'

'I've left her with Janvier.'

'Are you going to interrogate her yourself?'

'Not now. I don't know enough yet.'

'When are you planning to do it?'

'Tonight perhaps, or tomorrow, or the day after tomorrow.'

'And in the meantime?'

Maigret appeared so meek, so good-natured, that Coméliau wondered what he was up to.

'I've come to ask you what you've decided.'

'You can't keep her in an office indefinitely.'

'You're right, it's difficult. Especially with a woman.'

'Don't you think it's wise to put her in the cells?'

'That's for you to say.'

'Personally, would you release her?'

'I'm not sure what I would do.'

Frowning, Coméliau thought this over. He was angry. He finally said to Maigret, like a challenge:

'Send her to me.'

Why was Maigret smiling as he walked along the corridor? Was he imagining the conversation between Madame Calas and the exasperated magistrate?

He didn't see her again that afternoon. He merely went back into the inspectors' office and said to Torrence:

'Judge Coméliau is asking to see Madame Calas. Will you ask Janvier to deal with it?'

When the viscount saw him on the stairs and tried to grab hold of him, he got away by saying:

'Go and see Coméliau. I'm certain that he has, or will soon have, news for the press.'

He walked to the Brasserie Dauphine and stopped at the bar for an aperitif. It was late. Almost everyone had finished lunch. He picked up the telephone.

'Is that you?' he said to his wife.

'Aren't you coming home?'

'No.'

'I hope you have time to have some lunch?'

'I'm at the Brasserie Dauphine right now and I'm just about to.'

'Will you be here for dinner?'

'Maybe.'

Among the smells still hovering in the air, there were

two that dominated the others: Pernod, around the bar, and coq au vin wafting in from the kitchen.

Most of the tables were free in the dining room, where a few colleagues had got to the coffee and calvados stage. He hesitated, then finally remained standing and ordered a sandwich. The sun was as bright as it had been in the morning, the sky as clear, but a few white clouds were racing across it, and a breeze that had just risen raised the dust in the streets and stuck the women's dresses to their bodies.

The owner, who was behind the counter, knew Maigret well enough to know that now was not the time to engage him in conversation. Maigret ate distractedly, looking outside with the same gaze as the passengers of a boat watching the sea roll past, monotonous and hypnotic.

'Same again?'

He said yes, perhaps without knowing what he had been asked, ate his second sandwich and drank the coffee they had served him even though he hadn't ordered it.

A few minutes later, he was in a taxi taking him to Quai de Valmy. He stopped it on the corner of Rue des Récollets, opposite the lock, where three barges were waiting. In spite of the dirtiness of the water, with dubious-looking bubbles occasionally bursting on the surface, a few anglers, as always, were attaching their floats.

As he passed the yellow-painted facade of Popaul's, the owner recognized him. Maigret saw him through the window, pointing him out to a group of customers. A line of heavy goods lorries bearing the name 'Roulers and Langlois' were parked at the kerb.

Maigret passed a few shops, the kind found in all the working-class neighbourhoods of Paris. A fruit and vegetable display overflowed into the middle of the pavement. A little further on, there was a butcher's shop, empty of customers, then, very near Calas' bistro, a grocer's shop so dark it was impossible to make out anything inside.

Madame Calas had to leave home sometimes, even if only to do her shopping, and it was likely that she frequented these shops, in her slippers, with that thick black woollen shawl around her shoulders that he had noticed in the bistro.

Judel must have dealt with these people. The local police knew them, and were trusted by them more than anyone from Quai des Orfèvres could ever be.

The door of the bistro was locked. Sticking his forehead to the window, he could see nobody inside. In the kitchen, though, a figure occasionally caught a beam of sunlight. He knocked, had to knock again two or three times before Moers appeared, recognized him and rushed to the door.

'Sorry, we were making noise. Have you been waiting long?'

'It doesn't matter,' Maigret said, turning the key in the lock. 'Have you been disturbed a lot?'

'Some customers try to open and then go away. Others knock at the door and wave their arms insistently, demanding that we open up.'

Maigret looked around him, then went behind the counter to search for the kind of blotting pad he had seen on the table in the bedroom. Most bistros kept several of these, and he was surprised not to find a single one, whereas there were three boxes of dominoes, four or five baize covers and half a dozen packs of cards.

'Carry on,' he said to Moers. 'I'll speak to you later.'

He wormed his way between the equipment the technicians had set up in the kitchen and climbed to the first floor, from which he returned with the ink and the blotting paper.

Sitting at a table in the bistro, he wrote in capital letters:

Closed temporarily

He had hesitated before writing the second word, thinking perhaps of Coméliau, who right now was alone with Madame Calas.

'Have you seen any drawing pins anywhere?'

'On the left-hand shelf under the counter,' Moers replied from the kitchen.

He found them and went and stuck his notice to the crossbar of the door. When he turned, he felt something alive brushing against his leg and recognized the ginger cat, which turned its head towards him, looked at him and meowed.

It hadn't occurred to him. If the house was to stay empty for a while, the cat couldn't be left alone in it.

He went to the kitchen, found some milk in an earthenware jug and a cracked soup plate.

'I wonder who I can get to look after the cat.'

'Don't you think a neighbour would do it? I noticed a butcher's shop not far from here.'

'I'll ask them later. What have you found so far?'

They were combing the house, leaving no corner, no drawer unexplored. Moers would go first, examining objects with a magnifying glass, using if need be a portable microscope he had brought with him, and the photographers came after him.

'We started with the yard, which is the untidiest part of the house. It occurred to me they might have tried to hide something in all that mess.'

'I assume the dustbins have been emptied since Sunday?'

'Monday morning. We examined them anyway, looking for bloodstains, for instance.'

'Anything?'

'No, nothing,' Moers said, although he seemed hesitant.

That meant he had an idea but wasn't sure of it.

'What is it?'

'I don't know, chief. Just an impression. All three of us had the same thought. We were talking about it when you arrived.'

'Go on.'

'At least as far as the yard and kitchen are concerned, there's something strange. This isn't the kind of house where you'd expect to find everything spick and span. You just have to look in the drawers to see how untidy the place was. All sorts of things were stuffed in there, and most of them are covered in dust.'

Maigret, who was looking around him, thought he knew what Moers was getting at.

'Carry on,' he said with growing interest.

'Next to the sink, we found dishes from three days ago and saucepans that haven't been cleaned since Sunday. It's reasonable to assume this was normal, unless the wife had been neglecting the housework while the husband was away.'

Moers was right. The untidiness – even a degree of dirt – was probably customary.

'Logically we should have found a five- or ten-day layer of dirt everywhere. And yes, in some drawers, in some corners, there's dirt that's even older than that. But almost everywhere else it looks as if a lot of cleaning has been done recently. Sambois found two bottles of bleach in the yard. One of them's empty, and to judge by the state of the label it was bought recently.'

'When do you think this cleaning might have been done?'

'Three or four days ago. I'll be more specific in my report. Before that, I'll have to run a few tests in the lab.'

'What about fingerprints?'

'They confirm our theory. In the drawers and cupboards, we've found some of Calas'.'

'Are you sure?'

'They certainly match the prints from the body fished up from the canal.'

They finally had evidence that the dismembered man was indeed the owner of the bistro on Quai de Valmy.

'Are there similar prints upstairs?'

'Not on the furniture, only inside it. Dubois has studied the first floor in detail, we'll go back there later. What struck us is that there isn't a speck of dust on the furniture, and the floor has been carefully cleaned. As for the bedsheets, they haven't been used in the past three or four nights.'

'Have you found any dirty sheets anywhere?'

'I thought of that. No.'

'Did they do the washing at home?'

'I haven't seen any machine or any tub.'

'So they took dirty washing to a laundry.'

'Almost certainly yes. Now, unless the launderer came round yesterday or the day before . . .'

'I'm going to find out which laundry it is.'

Maigret was about to go and question one of the local shopkeepers. Stopping him, Moers opened a drawer in the kitchen sideboard.

'You have the name here.'

He showed him a wad of receipts, among which there were some from the Récollets Laundry. The most recent was from ten days earlier.

Maigret went to the phone booth, dialled the number and asked if any laundry had been collected from the bistro on Quai de Valmy that week.

'We only collect on Thursday morning,' he was told.

It was the previous Thursday that the last collection had been made.

Moers was right to be surprised. Two people couldn't have lived in the house since Thursday without producing some dirty linen, and it should have been somewhere, at least a few sheets, since those in the bedroom were almost clean.

Pensively, Maigret went back to the team.

'What were you saying about the prints?'

'So far, in the kitchen, we've found three sets, not count-ing yours and Lapointe's, which I know by heart. The most frequent are a woman's. I assume they're Madame Calas' prints.'

'That'll be easy to check.'

'Then there are the prints of a man I think is probably quite young. There are only a few of them, and they're the freshest ones.'

Antoine, presumably, whom Madame Calas must have given something to eat in the kitchen when he had arrived during the night.

'Finally, there are two prints from another man, includ-ing one partly erased.'

'Plus Calas' prints in the drawers?'

'Yes.'

'So to sum up, it looks as if quite recently, on Sunday, for example, the house was thoroughly cleaned, but nobody bothered about the inside of the furniture. Is that it?'

They were all thinking of the dismembered body that had been dragged up piece by piece from the waters of the canal.

That dismemberment hadn't been carried out in the street, or on a patch of waste ground. It had required time, because each piece had been carefully wrapped in news-paper and tied with string.

In what condition would a room be in after an operation like that had been performed in it?

Maigret now regretted having delivered Madame Calas into Judge Coméliau's far from gentle clutches.

'Have you been down to the cellar?'

'We had a quick look everywhere. At first glance, there's nothing unusual in the cellar, but we'll be going back down there, too.'

He left them to get on with their work. For a while, he walked up and down the bistro, and the ginger cat started following him. The sun lit the bottles lined up on the shelf and cast soft reflections on a corner of the counter. Passing the big stove, he realized that it had gone out. He opened it, saw that some of the ashes were still glowing and mechanically stirred them.

A moment later, he went behind the counter, dithered over the bottles, chose the bottle of calvados and poured himself a glass. The till was half open in front of him, with a few banknotes and some small change in it. On the wall to the right, near the window, hung a list of the drinks with their respective prices.

He took the price of a calvados from his pocket and put the money in the till. He jumped, as if caught out, when he saw a figure looming outside the window. It was Inspector Judel, who was trying to see inside.

Maigret went and opened the door.

'I thought I'd find you here, chief. I phoned headquarters and they told me they didn't know where you were.'

Judel looked around him with a touch of surprise, presumably searching for Madame Calas.

'Is it true you arrested her?'

'She's with Judge Coméliau.'

With his chin, Judel gestured towards the kitchen, where he could see the technicians.

'Have they found anything?'

'It's still too early to know.'

And, above all, too long to explain. Maigret didn't feel up to it.

'I'm glad I've got hold of you, I didn't want to do anything without your opinion. I think we've found the red-headed man.'

'Where is he?'

'If my information's correct, not far from here. Unless he's on night shift this week. He works as a timekeeper at Zenith Transport, the company that—'

'Rue des Récollets. I know. Roulers and Langlois.'

'I thought you'd prefer to question him yourself.'

Moers' voice reached them from the kitchen.

'Do you have a moment, chief?'

Maigret walked to the back of the bistro. Madame Calas' black shawl was spread on the table, and Moers, who had first examined it with a magnifying glass, was focusing his microscope.

'Want to have a look at this?'

'What am I looking for?'

'Do you see brownish lines on the wool that look like twigs? Actually, it's hemp. Our tests will confirm it, but I'm pretty sure. They're threads that are almost invisible to the naked eye and have come off a piece of string.'

'The same kind of string that . . .'

Maigret was referring to the string that had been used to wrap the parts of the dismembered body.

'I'd almost be prepared to swear it. Madame Calas probably didn't do a lot of wrapping. We haven't found a single piece of string like that in the house. There are pieces of string in a drawer, but it's either thinner string, or fibre string, or red string.'

'Many thanks. I assume you'll still be here when I get back?'

'What will you do with the cat?'

'Take him with me.'

The cat let itself be picked up, and Maigret was holding it under his arm as he left the house. He hesitated as he was about to enter the grocery and told himself that the animal would be better off in a butcher's shop.

'Isn't that Madame Calas' cat?' the butcher's wife asked as he approached the counter.

'Yes. Would it bother you to keep him for a few days?'

'As long as he doesn't fight with mine . . .'

'Is Madame Calas a customer of yours?'

'She comes in every morning. Is it true that it was her husband who . . .'

Instead of expressing herself in words on such a morbid subject she preferred to glance towards the canal.

'Yes, it looks like it's him.'

'What have they done with her?'

And as Maigret was searching for an evasive answer, she went on:

'I know that not everybody agrees with me and that there's a lot to be said about her, but as far as I'm concerned, she's an unhappy woman who's not to blame.'

Within a few minutes, the two men were waiting for the procession of lorries to pass so they could slip safely into the big yard of the Roulers and Langlois depot. A glass cage on the right bore the word 'Office' in black lettering.

The yard was surrounded by raised platforms that looked like the platforms in a railway freight yard, from which packages, sacks and crates were loaded into the lorries. There was an incessant rough and tumble of activity, and the noise was deafening.

'Chief!' Judel cried just as Maigret was reaching out for the door handle.

Maigret turned and saw a red-headed man standing on one of the platforms with a slim ledger in one hand, a pencil in the other, looking at them fixedly. He was of medium height and wore grey overalls. His shoulders were broad, and the skin of his face, bright, ruddy and pockmarked, looked like orange peel.

Men loaded with packages passed in front of him, each yelling a name, a number and the name of a town or village, but he didn't seem to hear them any longer, his blue eyes still fixed on Maigret.

'Don't let him get away,' Maigret told Judel.

He went into the office, where a young girl asked him what he wanted.

'Are either of the owners here?'

She didn't have to reply, because a man with close-cropped grey hair now came up to him, a questioning look on his face.

'Are you one of the owners?'

'Joseph Langlois. I get the feeling I've seen you somewhere before.'

He had probably seen his photograph in the newspapers. Maigret gave his name and Langlois waited suspiciously for what was to come next.

'Who's the red-headed man I can see on the other side of the yard?'

'What do you want with him?'

'I don't know yet. Who is he?'

'Dieudonné Pape, who's been working for me for more than twenty-five years. I'd be surprised if you found anything on him.'

'Is he married?'

'He's been a widower for years. Actually, I think his wife died only two or three years after they got married.'

'Does he live alone?'

'I suppose so. His private life is none of my business.'

'Do you have his address?'

'He lives in Rue des Écluses-Saint-Martin, not far from here. Do you know the number, Mademoiselle Berthe?'

'Fifty-six.'

'Does he work all day?'

'He does his eight hours, like everybody else, but not necessarily during the day. The depot is open day and night, lorries are loading and unloading constantly. Because of that, we have three shifts, and the rota changes every week.'

'What shift was he on last week?'

Langlois turned to the girl he had called Mademoiselle Berthe.

'Can you have a look?'

She checked in a file.

'The early shift.'

Langlois explained what this meant:

'In other words, he came on at six in the morning and finished at two in the afternoon.'

'Is your depot open on Sundays, too?'

'Yes, but with only two or three men on duty.'

'Was he one of them last Sunday?'

The girl again checked in her files.

'No.'

'What time is he due to finish today?'

'He's on the second shift. That means he'll knock off at ten this evening.'

'Could you get someone to take his place?'

'Can't you at least tell me what you want with him?'

'I'm sorry, I can't.'

'Is it something important?'

'Probably very important.'

'What do you suspect him of?'

'I prefer not to answer that.'

'Whatever you're thinking, I can tell you right now that you're barking up the wrong tree. If all my employees were like him, I'd never have anything to worry about.'

He wasn't pleased. Without telling Maigret what he was going to do and without asking him to follow him, he left the office, walked across the yard and went up to Dieudonné Pape.

Pape didn't react while his boss was talking to him, merely continued staring at the glass cage. Langlois turned to the far end of the yard and seemed to be calling someone. A little old man soon appeared, also in overalls, a pencil behind his ear. They exchanged a few words, and the newcomer took the ledger from the hands of the red-headed man, who followed his boss across the courtyard.

Maigret hadn't moved. The two men came in, and Langlois announced:

'This is a detective chief inspector from the Police Judiciaire. Apparently, he needs to speak to you.'

'I have a few questions for you, Monsieur Pape. If you don't mind coming with me . . .'

Dieudonné Pape pointed to his overalls.

'Can I change?'

'I'll go with you.'

Langlois didn't say goodbye to Maigret, who followed Pape into a kind of corridor that had been turned into a cloakroom. Pape didn't ask any questions. He must have been over fifty and gave the impression of a calm, meticulous man. He put on his coat and hat and walked out into the street with Judel on his right and Maigret on his left.

He seemed surprised that there was no car outside, as if he had expected to be taken immediately to Quai des Orfèvres. When they got to the corner of the street, opposite the yellow-painted bar, and they made him turn left instead of down towards the centre of the city, he opened his mouth to say something, but stopped in time.

Judel had realized that Maigret was taking them to Calas' bistro. The door was still locked, and Maigret knocked. Moers came and opened up for them.

'Go in, Pape.'

Maigret turned the key in the lock.

'You know this place well, don't you?'

The man was disorientated. While he might have foreseen that he would be questioned by the police, he was surprised by the way things were happening.

'You can take your coat off. The fire's on. Sit down in your place. I assume you have a regular seat?'

'I don't understand.'

'You know this place pretty well, don't you?'

'I'm a customer.'

He was trying to figure out what the men were doing in the kitchen with their equipment, and must also be wondering where Madame Calas was.

'A very good customer?'

'A good customer.'

'Did you come here on Sunday?'

He looked like an honest man, and there was both gentleness and shyness in his blue eyes, which were like the eyes of some animals which always seem to be wondering why human beings treat them so badly.

'Sit down.'

Intimidated, he did as he was told.

'I wasn't here on Sunday.'

He had thought before answering.

'Did you stay at home all day?'

'I went to see my sister.'

'Does she live in Paris?'

'No, in Nogent-sur-Marne.'

'Does she have a telephone?'

'Nogent 317. Her husband's a building contractor.'

'Did you see anyone else apart from your sister?'

'Her husband, her children, then, at about five, some

neighbours who are in the habit of coming to her house to play cards.'

Maigret signalled to Judel, who knew what he wanted and walked over to the phone booth.

'What time did you leave Nogent?'

'I took the eight o'clock bus.'

'Did you drop by here before going home?'

'No.'

'When did you last see Madame Calas?'

'On Saturday.'

'What shift were you on last week?'

'The morning shift.'

'So it was after two in the afternoon that you came here?'

'Yes.'

'Was Calas here?'

He had to think about this.

'Not when I arrived.'

'But he did come back?'

'I don't remember.'

'Did you stay here for a long time?'

'Quite a long time.'

'How long?'

'More than two hours. I don't know exactly.'

'What did you do?'

'I had a drink and chatted.'

'With other customers?'

'Mostly with Aline.'

He blushed as he uttered the name and hastened to explain:

'I think of her as a friend. We've known each other a long time.'

'How long?'

'More than ten years.'

'So you've been coming here every day for more than ten years?'

'Almost every day.'

'Preferably when her husband is away?'

This time, he didn't reply but bowed his head in a preoccupied manner.

'Are you her lover?'

'Who told you that?'

'It doesn't matter. Are you?'

Instead of replying, he asked anxiously:

'What have you done with her?'

Maigret replied openly:

'Right now she's with the examining magistrate.'

'Why?'

'To answer some questions about her husband's disappearance. Haven't you read the newspapers?'

As Dieudonné Pape didn't react, but remained lost in thought, Maigret called out:

'Moers! Can you take his prints?'

Pape let him take them. He seemed more concerned than scared, and his fingers didn't shake as they rested on the paper.

'Now compare them.'

'With which ones?'

'The two in the kitchen, including the one that's partly erased.'

When Moers walked away, Dieudonné Pape said in a soft but reproachful tone:

'If you want to know if I went in the kitchen, you only had to ask me. I often go there.'

'Were you there last Saturday?'

'I made myself a cup of coffee.'

'You don't know anything about the disappearance of Omer Calas?'

He still seemed to be thinking things over, like a man faced with a crucial decision.

'You don't know that he was murdered and his body dismembered and thrown in the canal?'

There was something quite impressive about it. Neither Judel nor Maigret had expected it. Slowly, the man turned to look at Maigret, appeared to scrutinize his face and at last said, still in the same soft but slightly reproachful voice:

'I have nothing to say.'

'Did you kill Calas?' Maigret insisted, with equal gravity.

Dieudonné Pape shook his head.

'I have nothing to say,' he repeated.

7. Madame Calas' Cat

Maigret was eating his dessert when he became aware of the way his wife was looking at him, a slightly sardonic but maternal smile on her lips. He pretended not to notice it at first, looked back down at his plate and ate a few more spoonfuls of egg custard before raising his eyes again.

'Do I have a mark on the end of my nose?' he grunted.

'No.'

'Then why are you laughing at me?'

'I'm not laughing. I'm smiling.'

'It's as if you're making fun of me. Am I so comical?'

'You're not comical, Jules.'

It was unusual for her to call him that, and it only happened when she was in a tender mood.

'What am I, then?'

'Do you realize you haven't said a single word since you've been sitting here?'

No, he hadn't realized.

'Could you even tell me what you've been eating?'

'Lamb's kidneys,' he replied in an artificially grouchy tone.

'And before?'

'Soup.'

'What kind of soup?'

'I don't know. Vegetable, I suppose.'

'Is that woman bothering you so much?'

Most of the time, and it was true of this case, too, Madame Maigret knew nothing of the cases her husband dealt with apart from what she read in the newspapers.

'Do you think she killed him?'

He shrugged like a man trying to rid himself of an obsession.

'I have no idea.'

'Or do you think Dieudonné Pape did it and she's his accomplice?'

He felt like telling her that it didn't matter. And indeed, as far as he was concerned, it didn't. What mattered was to understand. The fact was, not only did he not yet understand, the better he knew the people involved, the more in the dark he was.

The very reason he had come home for dinner instead of working away at his investigation was to clear his head, to plunge back into everyday life, as if to see the protagonists of the Quai de Valmy drama from another angle.

Instead of which, as his wife had remarked teasingly, he hadn't opened his mouth throughout the meal and had never for a moment stopped thinking about Madame Calas, Pape or, to a lesser degree, young Antoine.

It was unusual for him to feel so far from the solution to a problem, or more precisely for a problem to be posed in such an untechnical way.

There aren't many different types of crime. They can usually be put into three or four broad categories.

The crimes of professionals are merely a matter of

routine. That a criminal from the Corsican gang should kill a member of the Marseille gang in a bar in Rue de Douai is an almost mathematical problem for the men of the Police Judiciaire and can be solved with the help of an established procedure.

An attack by one or two young delinquents on a tobacconist or a bank cashier leads to a manhunt that also has its rules.

With a crime of passion, you know immediately where you're going.

Last but not least, with a crime committed for financial gain, one involving an inheritance, a life insurance policy or some more complicated plan to get hold of the victim's money, you're on safe ground as soon as you've discovered the motive.

That was how Judge Coméliau saw this case, perhaps because he couldn't admit that the private lives of people belonging to a world different from his, especially the inhabitants of Quai de Valmy, could be at all complicated.

If Dieudonné Pape was Madame Calas' lover, then Dieudonné Pape and Madame Calas had got rid of her husband, both to be free and to get their hands on his money.

'They've been lovers for more than ten years,' Maigret had retorted. 'Why would they have waited all this time?'

The judge dismissed the objection with a gesture. Calas might have received a large sum of money from somewhere, or else the lovers had been waiting for the right opportunity, or else Madame Calas and her husband had quarrelled and Madame Calas had decided she'd had enough. Or else . . .

'What if we discover that apart from his bistro, which isn't worth much, Calas didn't have any money?'

'Then there's still the bistro. Dieudonné had enough of working for Zenith Transport and decided to spend the rest of his days putting his feet up in the warm atmosphere of a little place like that.'

That was the one objection that had swayed Maigret a little.

'What about Antoine Cristin?'

It was true: the judge now had two possible culprits to consider rather than one. Cristin was also Madame Calas' lover, and he was more likely than Pape to have needed money.

'The other two used him. You'll see, we'll discover that he was their accomplice.'

That was what the story had become in moving from Quai de Valmy to an examining magistrate's office. And until the truth came to light, all three of them were under lock and key.

What made Maigret even surlier, even angrier with himself, was that he hadn't tried to resist Coméliau, had given in immediately, out of laziness or fear of complications.

Ever since the start of his career, he had learned from his elders, then from his own experience, that you should never question a suspect in depth before you've built up a clear picture of the case. An interrogation is not about throwing out hypotheses haphazardly, constantly telling someone he's guilty and hoping that after hammering away at him for a certain number of hours he'll confess.

Even the most short-sighted of suspects has a kind of sixth sense and can immediately sense if the police are making random accusations or have something solid to go on.

Maigret had always preferred to wait. Sometimes, in difficult cases, when he didn't feel sure of himself, he actually preferred to leave a suspect at large for as long as was necessary, even if that meant taking a bit of a risk.

It had always worked.

'Contrary to what people might suppose,' he liked to say, 'a suspect feels a kind of relief when he's arrested, because now he knows where he stands. He no longer has to wonder if he's being followed, if he's being watched, if he's under suspicion, if a trap is being set for him. He's accused, and he defends himself. And now he benefits from the protection of the law. In prison, he becomes an almost sacred person, and everything that's done to build up a case against him will have to be done according to a number of specific rules.'

Aline Calas had been a good example of this. Once in the magistrate's office, she had hardly opened her mouth. Coméliau hadn't got anything more from her than from one of the stones transported by the Naud brothers.

'I have nothing to say,' she kept saying in a neutral voice, adding when he bombarded her with questions: 'You have no right to interrogate me without a lawyer present.'

'Then tell me the name of your lawyer.'

'I don't have one.'

'Here's a list of members of the Paris Bar. Choose a name.'

'I don't know them.'

'Choose one at random.'

'I don't have any money.'

They were forced to appoint a lawyer, which entailed various formalities and took some time.

Coméliau had had young Antoine brought in, late in the afternoon. Having withstood Lapointe's questioning for hours, he wasn't going to be any more forthcoming with the magistrate.

'I didn't kill Monsieur Calas. I didn't go to Quai de Valmy on Saturday afternoon. I didn't leave a suitcase in the left luggage office at Gare de l'Est. The man's either lying or mistaken.'

Meanwhile, his mother was waiting in the corridor of the Police Judiciaire, red-eyed, holding a handkerchief rolled into a ball. Lapointe had spoken to her, and so had Lucas. She insisted on waiting, repeating that she wanted to see Detective Chief Inspector Maigret.

That often happened with simple people, who assume they won't get anywhere with subordinates and are determined to talk to the boss.

Maigret couldn't have seen her at that moment, because he was just leaving the bistro on Quai de Valmy with Judel and Dieudonné Pape.

'Will you close up and bring the key to headquarters?' he said to Moers.

All three had crossed the footbridge to Quai de Jemmapes. Rue des Écluses-Saint-Martin was not far, in a quiet area behind the Hôpital Saint-Louis that had something of a provincial air about it. Pape hadn't been handcuffed. Maigret had judged that he wasn't the kind of man who'd try to run away.

He was calm and dignified, as calm in his way as Madame Calas. He didn't seem so much defeated as sad, with a hint of what looked like resignation.

He didn't talk much. He probably never talked much. He answered questions in as few words as possible and occasionally didn't answer at all, merely looking at Maigret with his lavender-blue eyes.

He lived in an old five-storey building with a comfortable, lower-middle-class air to it. As they passed the lodge, the concierge stood up and watched them through the window. They didn't stop, but climbed to the second floor, where Pape opened the door on the left with his key.

His apartment consisted of three rooms, a dining room, a bedroom and a kitchen, as well as a kind of junk room that had been turned into a bathroom and in which Maigret was quite surprised to find a bathtub. Although not modern, the furniture was less old-fashioned than in the Calas house, and everything was remarkably clean.

'Do you have a cleaning lady?' Maigret had asked with surprise.

'No.'

'Do you do the cleaning yourself?'

Dieudonné Pape couldn't help but smile with satisfaction, proud of his home.

'Doesn't the concierge ever come up and lend you a hand?'

Beyond the kitchen window hung a well-stocked food safe.

'You also make your own meals?'

'Always.'

Above the chest of drawers in the dining room hung an enlarged photograph of Madame Calas in a gilded frame, so similar to those found in most households that it gave the apartment a cosy, conjugal feel.

Remembering that he hadn't found any photographs in the Calas house, Maigret had asked:

'How did you get hold of this?'

'I took it with my camera and had it enlarged on Boulevard Saint-Martin.'

The camera was in a drawer in the chest. In a corner of the bathroom was a little table covered in glass tubs and flasks filled with products used for developing.

'Do you do a lot of photography?'

'Yes. Especially landscapes.'

It was true. Searching the furniture, Maigret had found a batch of photographs depicting different parts of Paris, and a smaller number of countryside views. Many showed the canal and the Seine. For most of them, Dieudonné Pape must have had to wait a long time in order to obtain certain quite striking lighting effects.

'Which suit did you wear to visit your sister?'

'The navy-blue.'

He owned three suits, including the one he was wearing now.

'Take them with you,' Maigret had said to Judel. 'The shoes, too.'

And finding dirty washing in a wicker basket, he'd had it added to the rest.

He had noticed a canary hopping in a cage, but it wasn't until they were on their way out that he thought about what might happen to it.

'Do you know anyone who'll agree to have him?'

'I'm sure the concierge will be glad to.'

Maigret had taken the cage and stopped outside. He didn't even need to knock.

'Don't tell me you're taking him away?' the concierge had exclaimed angrily.

She wasn't talking about the canary, but about her tenant. She had recognized Judel, who was local. She might well have recognized Maigret, too. And she had read the newspapers.

'To treat a man like him, the best man in the world, like a common criminal!'

She was short, dark and slovenly-looking, with a shrill voice. She was so angry, it looked as if she might scratch.

'Could you look after the canary for a while?'

She had literally torn the cage from his hands.

'Just wait and see what the tenants and neighbours say! And don't worry, Monsieur Dieudonné, we'll all visit you in prison.'

Once past a certain age, working-class women often worship bachelors or widowers like Dieudonné Pape, admiring their well-ordered lives. When the three men walked away, she was still on the pavement, weeping and waving goodbye.

Maigret had said to Judel:

'Take the clothes and shoes to Moers. He'll know what to do with them. And I want the house on Quai de Valmy kept under surveillance.'

He was ordering this surveillance for no specific reason, more to avoid any possible reproach in the future than for anything else. Meekly, Dieudonné Pape waited at the kerb. Then he fell into step with Maigret, and the two of them walked along the quayside in search of a taxi.

In the cab, he said nothing, and Maigret, for his part, avoided asking any questions. Filling his pipe, he held it out to Pape.

'Do you smoke a pipe?'

'No.'

'Cigarettes?'

'I don't smoke.'

He did ask one question, though, one that seemed to have no connection with Calas' death.

'Do you drink?'

'No.'

It was a further anomaly. Maigret found it hard to fit that in with everything else. Madame Calas was an alcoholic and had started drinking years ago, probably even before meeting Pape.

It's quite rare for someone who has a craving for drink to stand the presence of a teetotaller.

Maigret had known couples quite similar to the one formed by Madame Calas and Dieudonné Pape. In every case he could remember, both the man and the woman were big drinkers.

He had been pondering all this over dinner,

unconsciously, while his wife watched him without his realizing it. He had thought of many other things, too.

Antoine's mother, for instance, whom he had found waiting in the corridor of the Police Judiciaire and admitted to his office. He had already handed Pape over to Lucas with the words:

'Tell Coméliau he's here. If he asks to see him, take him there. Otherwise, take him to the cells.'

Without reacting, Pape had followed Lucas into one of the offices while Maigret walked away with the woman.

'I swear to you, inspector, my son can't possibly have done that. He wouldn't harm a fly. He tries to act tough, because that's the fashion with young men these days. But I know him, I know he's only a child.'

'I believe you, madame.'

'So if you believe me, why won't you let me have him back? I promise you I won't let him go out in the evening any more and I'll stop him seeing women. When I think that woman is almost the same age as me and has no shame about taking up with a boy who's young enough to be her son! I'd sensed for a while that there was something going on. When I saw him buying products for his hair, cleaning his teeth twice a day and even putting on scent, I told myself . . .'

'Is he your only child?'

'Yes. And I take particular care of him because his father died of TB. I've done everything for him, inspector. If only I could see him, talk to him! Do you think they'll let me? They can't stop a mother from seeing her son, can they?'

All he could do was send her to see Coméliau. It was a bit cowardly, he knew, but he had no choice. She must have waited on another bench in the corridor upstairs, and Maigret didn't know if the magistrate had finally agreed to see her.

Moers had got back to headquarters just before six o'clock and handed over the key to the Calas house, a big old-fashioned key that Maigret now had in his pocket along with the key to Pape's apartment.

'Did Judel let you have the clothes, the shoes and the linen?'

'Yes. I have them in the lab. I assume I should be looking for bloodstains?'

'That in particular. Tomorrow morning, I may send you to his apartment.'

'I'll come back here and work this evening after I've had a bite to eat. I assume it's urgent?'

It was always urgent. The more time you take on a case, the less fresh the leads, and the more time people have had to prepare their defence.

'Will you come up this evening?'

'I don't know. When you leave, drop a note on my desk.'

Now he stood up from the dining table and filled his pipe, like a man who doesn't know what to do with himself, then looked uncertainly at his armchair.

'How about giving your mind a rest just for one evening?' Madame Maigret ventured. 'Stop thinking about your case. Read something, or if you like let's go to the cinema, and tomorrow morning you'll wake up with a clear head.'

He gave her a sardonic look.

'You want to go to the cinema?'

'There's quite a good film playing at the Moderne.'

She served him his coffee, and, if he'd had a coin to hand, he would have been tempted to toss it to decide what to do with his evening.

Madame Maigret took care not to hurry him, to let him sip at his coffee. He strode up and down the dining room, stopping every now and again to stare at the carpet.

'No!' he at last said, resolutely.

'Are you going out?'

'Yes.'

Before putting on his coat, he poured himself a little glass of sloe gin.

'Will you be back late?'

'I don't know. It's unlikely.'

Perhaps because he didn't have the impression that what he was going to do was important enough, he didn't take a taxi, nor did he call Quai des Orfèvres and ask for one of the police cars. He walked to the Métro, took a train and got out at Château-Landon.

The neighbourhood had put on its unsettling night-time face, with shadowy figures hugging the buildings, women motionless at the kerb and murky lighting in the bars that made them look like fish tanks.

A man standing not far from the Calas' door rushed forwards when Maigret stopped and shone a torch in his face.

'Oh, sorry, inspector! I didn't recognize you in the dark.'

It was one of Judel's officers.

'Anything to report?'

'No. Or rather, yes. I don't know if it's of any importance. About an hour ago, a taxi came along the quayside and started slowing down about fifty metres away. It kept going, slowing even more as it got to the house, but didn't stop.'

'Did you see who was inside?'

'A woman. When the cab passed the streetlamp, I saw that she was young. She had a grey coat on, no hat. Then the taxi sped up again and turned left into Rue Louis-Blanc.'

Was it Lucette, Madame Calas' daughter, who had come to check that her mother hadn't been released? She knew from the newspapers that she had been taken to Quai des Orfèvres, but so far the press hadn't said anything more.

'Do you think she saw you?'

'It's quite likely. Judel didn't say anything about having to hide. Most of the time, I walk up and down to keep warm.'

There was another possibility. Had Lucette Calas intended to go inside the house if it wasn't being watched? To get what, if that was the case?

He shrugged, took the key from his pocket and turned it in the lock. He couldn't immediately find the light switch, not having had occasion to use it before. A single light came on, and he had to go to the bar, where there was another switch, in order to turn on the light at the far end.

Moers and his men had tidied everything before they left, so that there was nothing changed in the bistro, except that the stove had finally gone out and the place felt colder. As he was walking towards the kitchen, Maigret jumped, because something had just moved noiselessly near him. It took him a few seconds to realize that it was the cat he had earlier left with the butcher's wife.

The animal now rubbed against his leg, and Maigret bent down to stroke it.

'How did you get in here?' he muttered.

It bothered him. The door that led from the kitchen to the yard was locked. The window was also closed. He went upstairs, switched on the light on the first floor and found a half-open window. Now he understood. There was a shed in the yard of the neighbouring house, a shed with a zinc roof, and it was from there that the cat had jumped, a distance of more than two metres.

Maigret went back downstairs. As there was a little milk left in the earthenware jug, he gave it to the cat.

'What now?' he said aloud, as if talking to the cat.

What must they look like, the two of them, there in the empty house?

He had never realized how solitary and desolate a bistro could look, without the owner behind the counter, without customers. Yes, this was how the room looked every night once the last customers had gone and Calas had put up the shutters and turned the key in the lock.

They were both there then, he and his wife, and there was nothing left to do but turn out the lights, walk through the kitchen and go upstairs to bed. Madame Calas was most often in a state of dazed lethargy from all the swigs of cognac she'd taken during the day.

Did she have to hide from her husband to drink? Or else, pleased with the outside recreations he himself enjoyed every afternoon, did he treat his wife's passion for the bottle with indulgence?

It suddenly occurred to Maigret that there was one person about whom they knew almost nothing, and that was the dead man. From the first, for everyone, he had been the dismembered man. An odd thing, which Maigret had often noticed, was that people don't have the same reactions, the same pity for example, or the same revulsion, faced with scattered limbs as opposed to an intact corpse. It is as if the dead person becomes more anonymous, almost comical, and you're lucky if they don't smile when they talk about it.

He hadn't seen Calas' head, which still hadn't been found and might never be found, or a photograph of him.

The man was from a peasant background, short and thickset. Every year, he went to buy wine from vineyards around Poitiers. He wore quite thin woollen suits and played billiards in the afternoon somewhere near Gare de l'Est.

Apart from his wife, was there a woman in his life? Were there several? Was he unaware of what happened in his own house when he was away?

He must have met Pape and, if he had even the slightest insight, had surely guessed at the relationship that had developed between that man and his wife.

Both gave the impression, not so much of a couple of lovers, but rather of an already old relationship, people united by a deep, calm feeling, founded on mutual understanding and indulgence, that particular tenderness only encountered in couples of a certain age who have a lot to forgive each other for.

If he knew that, was he resigned to it? Did he turn a blind eye or, on the contrary, did he quarrel with his wife?

What was his reaction to the others, those like young Antoine, who sneaked in and took advantage of Aline Calas' weakness? Did he know about that, too?

Maigret had finally headed for the bar, and his hand hesitated among the bottles of spirits, finally grabbed a bottle of calvados. It struck him that he mustn't forget to put some money in the till. The cat had gone and sat down near the stove and, instead of falling asleep, was restless, surprised at feeling no warmth.

Maigret could understand the relationship between Madame Calas and Pape. He could understand Antoine, too, and the ones who merely passed through.

What he didn't understand was Calas and his wife. How and why had they got together, then married, lived together for so many years and even had a daughter whom they seemed to have lost interest in, as if she had nothing in common with them?

There was no photograph to enlighten him, no correspondence, none of those things in a house that make it possible to get an idea of the state of mind of those living in it.

He finished his drink and poured himself another. He was in a bad mood. Glass in hand, he went and sat down at the table where he had seen Madame Calas sit as if it was her usual place.

He knocked his pipe against his heel, filled another, lit it, his eyes fixed on the counter, the glasses, the bottles. He wondered now if he wasn't in the process of finding the answer to his question, or at least part of his question.

When it came down to it, what did the house consist of? A kitchen where nobody ate, because the couple had their meals at the table at the far end of the bistro, and a bedroom where they did nothing but sleep.

Whether it was Calas or his wife, it was here that they lived, in the bistro, which for them was what the dining room or living room is in an ordinary household.

When the couple had arrived in Paris, hadn't they almost immediately settled on Quai de Valmy, never to move from it?

Maigret even had the impression that this, too, shed a new light on the relationship between Madame Calas and Dieudonné Pape, and he smiled.

It was still quite vague and he would have been unable to express his thoughts in clear sentences. All the same, he was losing the sluggishness that had been affecting him for the last few hours. Finishing his drink, he went to the phone booth and dialled the number of the cells.

'Detective Chief Inspector Maigret here. Who am I speaking to? . . . Joris? How's your new customer? . . . Yes, the Calas woman, as you call her . . . What? And what did you do?'

He felt sorry for her. She had called the guard twice. Both times, she had tried to persuade him to bring her a little brandy, promising to pay him any amount of money.

It hadn't occurred to Maigret how much she would suffer from being deprived of it.

'No, of course not . . .'

He couldn't tell Joris to give her some in spite of the regulations. Maybe he would bring her some himself tomorrow morning, or give her some in his office?

'I'd like you to look in the papers that were taken from her. Her identity card must be there. I know she comes from somewhere near Gien, but I can't remember the name of the village.'

He had to wait quite a long time.

'What? . . . Boissancourt, near Saint-André. Boissancourt with an *a*? . . . Thanks, my friend! Goodnight! Don't be too hard on her.'

He called Directory Inquiries and gave his name.

'Would you be so kind, mademoiselle, as to find me Boissancourt, near Saint-André, between Montargis and Gien, and read me out the list of subscribers.'

'Will you stay on the line?'

'Yes.'

It didn't take long. The woman was excited at the thought of assisting the famous Detective Chief Inspector Maigret.

'Are you taking this down?'

'Yes.'

'Aillevard, Route des Chênes, unemployed.'

'Go on.'

'Ancelin, Victor, butcher. Don't you want the number?'

'No.'

'Honoré de Boissancourt, chateau of Boissancourt.'

'Go on.'

'Dr Camuzet.'

'Give me his number.'

'17.'

'Next?'

'Calas, Robert, cattle merchant.'

'Number?'

'21.'

'Calas, Julien, grocer. His number is 3.'

'Any other Calases?'

'No. There's a Louchez, who's unemployed, a Pied-bœuf, who's a blacksmith, and a Simonin, who's a grain merchant.'

'Could you call me the first Calas on the list, then probably the second one as well?'

He heard the telephone girls talking to each other down the line, then a voice announced:

'Saint-André on the line.'

Number 21 was rung. The ringing went on for a long time until a woman's voice was heard.

'What is it?'

'Detective Chief Inspector Maigret here, from the Police Judiciaire in Paris. Are you Madame Calas? Is your husband at home?'

He was in bed with flu.

'Are you related to a man named Omer Calas?'

'What's he been up to? Has he done something wrong?'

'So you know him?'

'Actually, I've never seen him, because I'm not from here, I'm from the Haute-Loire, and he'd already gone when I married.'

'Is he a relative of your husband's?'

'His first cousin. He still has a brother around here, Julien, who's a grocer.'

'Do you know anything else about him?'

'About Omer? No, and I have no desire to know anything more.'

She must have hung up, because another voice asked:

'Do you want me to put the second call through, inspector?'

This time, the answer came more quickly. The man who came on the line was even more reticent.

'I hear what you're saying. But what exactly do you want of me?'

'Was Omer Calas your brother?'

'I had a brother named Omer.'

'Is he dead?'

'I have no idea. I haven't heard from him in twenty, almost twenty-five years.'

'A man named Omer Calas has been murdered in Paris.'

'I heard that earlier on the radio.'

'Did you also hear his description? Does he sound like your brother?'

'After so long, it's hard to say.'

'Did you know he lived in Paris?'

'No.'

'Or that he was married?'

Silence.

'Do you know his wife?'

'Listen. I have nothing to tell you. I was fifteen when

my brother left. I haven't seen him since. I've never had a letter from him. I have no desire to know. If you want information, you should call Maître Canonge.'

'Who's he?'

'The lawyer.'

When he finally got hold of Canonge's number, the man's wife exclaimed:

'Well, that's a coincidence!'

'What is?'

'That you should be phoning now. How did you know? Earlier, after hearing the news on the radio, my husband wondered if he should phone you or go to see you. In the end, he decided to go to Paris. He took the 8.22 train. He'll be at Gare d'Austerlitz just after midnight, I don't know the exact time.'

'Where does he usually stay?'

'In the old days, the train arrived at Gare d'Orsay. He still stays at the Hôtel d'Orsay.'

'What does your husband look like?'

'A handsome man, tall, strong, with grey hair. He's wearing a brown coat, a brown suit, and, apart from his briefcase, he took a pigskin suitcase with him. I'm still wondering what it was that made you think of him.'

When Maigret hung up, he had a smug smile on his face in spite of himself and almost poured himself another drink. Then he told himself he would have plenty of time for a drink at the station.

All that remained was to telephone Madame Maigret and tell her he would be back quite late tonight.

8. The Lawyer from Saint-André

Madame Canonge hadn't exaggerated. Her husband really was a handsome man of about sixty who looked more like a gentleman farmer than a country lawyer. Standing by the gate at the end of the platform, Maigret immediately recognized him from a distance as he strode among the passengers from the 12.22 train, towering over the others, a pigskin suitcase in one hand, his briefcase in the other, and it was clear from his self-confident demeanour that he was a regular in this station and even on that train.

Tall and strong, he was the only one to be dressed with an almost overly studied elegance. His overcoat wasn't just any brown, but an unusual soft chestnut colour that Maigret had never seen, and the cut bore the mark of a high-class tailor.

His complexion was ruddy beneath his silvery hair, and even in the bad light of the station forecourt Maigret could tell this was a man who took good care of himself. He was closely shaven and probably wore a discreet eau de Cologne.

Some fifty metres from the gate, he had spotted Maigret among the people waiting and had frowned, like a man trying to remember something. He, too, must often have seen the inspector's photograph in the newspapers.

Coming closer, he was still unsure whether or not to smile and hold out his hand.

It was Maigret who took two steps forwards.

'Maître Canonge?'

'Yes. Are you Detective Chief Inspector Maigret?'

He put his suitcase down at his feet and shook the proffered hand.

'You're not going to tell me you're here by chance?'

'No. I phoned your house this evening. Your wife told me you'd taken the train and that you'd be staying at the Hôtel d'Orsay. To be on the safe side, I thought it best to come here and wait for you.'

There was still one thing the lawyer didn't understand.

'Did you read my ad?'

'No.'

'Strange! Before anything else, I think we should get out of here. Will you come with me to the Hôtel d'Orsay?'

They took a taxi.

'I came to Paris to see you and was planning to phone you first thing tomorrow.'

Maigret had not been mistaken. His companion gave off a slight aroma of eau de Cologne and good cigars.

'Have you put Madame Calas in prison?'

'Judge Coméliau has signed an arrest warrant.'

'It's a remarkable story . . .'

They drove along the river. A few minutes later, they pulled up outside the Hôtel d'Orsay, where the doorman greeted the lawyer like an old guest.

'I don't suppose the restaurant is still open, Alfred?'

'No, Monsieur Canonge.'

'Before the war, when all the Paris–Orléans trains arrived here,' Canonge explained to Maigret, who knew it perfectly well, 'the station restaurant stayed open all night. It was practical. I don't suppose you really want to talk in a hotel room, do you? How about going for a drink somewhere?'

They had to walk quite some way along Boulevard Saint-Germain to find a brasserie still open.

'What are you drinking, inspector?'

'A beer.'

'Could you bring me your finest brandy, waiter?'

Both of them, having taken off their coats and hats, sat down on the banquette. While Maigret lit his pipe, Canonge cut the end off his cigar with a silver pocket knife.

'I don't suppose you've ever been to Saint-André?'

'No, never.'

'It's off the main road and there's nothing to attract tourists. If I understood correctly what the radio announced this afternoon, the dismembered man from the Canal Saint-Martin is none other than that rascal Calas?'

'His fingerprints match those found in the house on Quai de Valmy.'

'When I read the few lines the newspapers devoted to the discovery of the body, I had a feeling it was him and I almost phoned you.'

'Did you know Calas?'

'I used to. I knew the woman who became his wife rather better. Cheers! What I'm wondering now is where to begin. It's a more complicated story than you might think. Has Aline Calas mentioned me?'

'No.'

'Do you believe she's mixed up in the murder of her husband?'

'I don't know. The examining magistrate is convinced she is.'

'What has she said in her defence?'

'Nothing.'

'Has she confessed?'

'No. She refuses to say a word.'

'I think, inspector, that she's the most extraordinary person I've ever met in my life. And yet the countryside is full of eccentric characters, I can assure you.'

He must have been used to being listened to and he clearly liked the sound of his own voice. He held his cigar between his well-tended fingers in a pose that must have been personal to him, one that displayed his gold signet ring.

'I'd better begin at the beginning. Obviously you've never heard of Honoré de Boissancourt?'

Maigret shook his head.

'He is, or rather he was until a month ago, the richest man in our region. Apart from the chateau of Boissancourt, he owned about fifteen farms comprising 2,000 hectares in all, plus a good thousand hectares of woods and two lakes. If you're familiar with the provinces, you probably get the idea.'

'I was born in the country.'

Not only had Maigret been born in the country, but his father had been the manager of a similar estate.

'Now, it's useful for you to know who this Boissancourt

was. For that, I have to go back to his grandfather, whom my father, who was also a lawyer in Saint-André, already knew. His name wasn't Boissancourt but Dupré, Christophe Dupré. The son of a tenant farmer, he first established himself as a cattle merchant and was tough and crafty enough to quickly amass a fortune. I suppose you know that kind of man, too.'

Listening to him, Maigret felt somewhat as if he was reliving his own childhood. In the region he came from, there had been someone like Christophe Dupré, who had become one of the richest men in the country and whose son was now a senator.

'After a while, Dupré started buying and selling corn. His speculating made him a lot of money. With his profits, he bought land, one farm at first, then two, then three, so that by the time he died, the chateau of Boissancourt, which used to belong to a widow without children, had passed into his hands along with its outbuildings. Christophe had married the daughter of a cavalry officer and they had one son and one daughter. When he died, his son, Alain, started to call himself Dupré de Boissancourt. Gradually, he dropped the Dupré and eventually, when he was elected to the departmental council, he obtained a decree legalizing his new name.'

This, too, brought many memories back to Maigret's mind.

'So much for the older generations. Honoré de Boissancourt, the grandson of Christophe Dupré, who could be called the founder of the dynasty, died a month ago. He'd married Emilie d'Espissac, from an old local family that had fallen on hard times. After giving him a daughter, she died in a riding accident when the child was still very young. I knew her well, a charming woman, who bore her own ugliness with melancholy and who had let herself be sacrificed by her parents without protest. It was claimed that Boissancourt gave them a million, to buy her, so to speak. As the family lawyer, I can tell you the figure is exaggerated, but it's true all the same that old Comtesse d'Espissac received a large sum the day the contract was signed.'

'What kind of man was the last Boissancourt?'

'I'm getting to that. I was his lawyer. For years, I dined at the chateau once a week and I've always hunted on his lands. So I knew him well. First of all, he had a club foot, which may partly explain why he was so gloomy and touchy. No doubt the fact that everybody knew the history of his family and most of the chateaux in the region were closed to him didn't help to make him any more sociable.

'His whole life, he had the impression that people despised him and were conspiring to rob him, so he was always on the defensive, in anticipation of being attacked.

'He took over a turret in the chateau and turned it into a kind of study where, for days on end, he'd go over the accounts, not only those of his tenant farmers and gamekeepers, but every one of his suppliers, correcting the butcher's and grocer's figures in red ink. He'd often go down to the kitchen when the servants were having their meals, to make sure they weren't being served expensive dishes.

'I don't suppose there's anything wrong in my betraying what were professional confidences between us. Anyone in Saint-André could tell you the same thing.'

'Is Madame Calas his daughter?'

'You guessed it.'

'And Omer Calas?'

'He worked at the chateau for four years as a manservant. He was the son of an alcoholic day labourer who didn't amount to much. This all goes back twenty-five years.'

He signalled to a passing waiter and said to Maigret:

'This time, will you have a brandy with me? Two brandies, waiter! Obviously,' he went on as soon as he turned back to Maigret, 'you couldn't have surmised all this just from visiting the bistro on Quai de Valmy.'

That wasn't entirely correct, and Maigret wasn't in the least surprised by what he was learning.

'I sometimes talked about Aline with old Dr Pétrelle, who's sadly dead now and has been replaced by Camuzet. Camuzet never knew her and won't be able to tell you anything about her. As for me, I'm incapable of describing her case to you in technical terms.

'Even when she was a small child, she was different from the other little girls. There was something disturbing about her. She never played with anyone else, didn't go to school either, because her father was determined for her to have a private tutor. She didn't have just one, but a dozen at least, because the child saw to it that she made life impossible for them.

'Did she hold her father responsible for the fact that she led an existence different from other people? Or was it much more complicated than that, as Pétrelle claimed? I have no idea. Most girls, it seems, love their fathers, sometimes to an exaggerated extent. I have no experience of that, because my wife and I don't have children. Can that kind of love turn to hate?

'Be that as it may, she seemed to take a delight in being the bane of Boissancourt's life. At the age of twelve, she was caught trying to set fire to the chateau.

'Fire was her obsession for quite a while, and they were forced to keep a close eye on her.

'Then there was Omer, who was five or six years older than her and was then what the peasants call a strapping lad, sturdy, tough, with an insolent gleam in his eye as soon as his employer had his back turned.'

'Did you see what happened between them?' Maigret asked, looking absently around the almost empty brasserie, where the waiters were waiting for the last customers to leave.

'Not at the time. Again, it was Pétrelle who told me this. According to him, she must have started taking an interest in Omer when she was no more than thirteen or fourteen. That happens to other girls that age, but it usually stays quite vague and more or less platonic.

'Was it any different with her? Did Calas, who wasn't exactly scrupulous, take advantage more than men usually do in such cases?

'Whatever the truth of it, Pétrelle was convinced that they conducted a dubious relationship over a long period of time. He put it down largely to Aline's need to defy her father, to disappoint him.

'It's possible. It's not my field. The only reason I'm going into all these details is to make the rest more comprehensible.

'One day, when she wasn't yet seventeen, she went to see the doctor in secret and asked to be examined. He confirmed that she was pregnant.'

'How did she take it?' Maigret asked.

'Pétrelle told me she looked him straight in the face and said between her teeth: "All the better!"'

'What you should know is that in the meantime, Calas had married the butcher's daughter, because she was pregnant, too, and she'd given him a child a few weeks earlier. He was still working as a manservant at the chateau, because he had no other trade, and his wife was living with her parents.

'One Sunday, the village learned that Aline de Boissancourt and Omer Calas had disappeared. According to the servants, there had been a dramatic scene the previous evening between the girl and her father. For more than two hours, they'd been heard arguing loudly in the small drawing room.

'To the best of my knowledge, Boissancourt never tried to find his daughter. And as far as I know, she never wrote to him either.

'As for Calas' first wife, she became a depressive. She survived for another three years until she was found swinging from a tree in the orchard.'

The waiters had piled up the chairs on most of the tables, and one of them was looking at Maigret and Canonge and holding a big silver watch in his hand.

'I think we ought to let them close,' Maigret said.

Canonge insisted on paying for the drinks and they left. The night was cool, the sky starry, and they walked for a while in silence. It was Canonge who said:

'Maybe we could find another place open for one last drink?'

Each deep in his own thoughts, they walked along much of Boulevard Raspail until they spotted a little nightclub in Montparnasse. The lights outside were blue, and music could be heard wafting out from inside.

'Shall we go in?'

Instead of letting themselves be led to a table, they sat down at the bar, where two girls were hard at work on a fat man who was more than half drunk.

'The same again?' Canonge asked, taking another cigar from his pocket.

A few couples were dancing. Two girls left the other end of the room and came and sat down next to them, but Maigret gestured them away, and they didn't insist.

'There are still Calases in Boissancourt and Saint-André,' Canonge said.

'I know. A cattle merchant and a grocer.'

Canonge gave a little laugh. 'It would be funny if the cattle merchant became rich enough in his turn to buy the chateau and the land! One of the Calases is Omer's brother, the other his cousin. He also has a sister who married a gendarme in Gien. When Boissancourt had a brain haemorrhage a month ago, just as he was sitting down to eat, I went to see all three of them to find out if they'd heard from Omer.'

'Hold on,' Maigret cut in. 'Didn't Boissancourt disown his daughter?'

'Everyone in the area was convinced he had. People were wondering who was going to inherit the property, because in a village like that, everyone more or less depends on the chateau.'

'I assume you knew?'

'No. In his last years, Boissancourt made several wills, all of them different, but never gave them to me for safe-keeping. He must have torn them up one by one because none of them were found.'

'In other words, his daughter inherits his property?'

'Automatically.'

'So you put an ad in the newspapers?'

'Yes, as is usual in such cases. I couldn't put the name Calas in it, since I didn't know if they were married. Not many people read those kinds of ads. I didn't think it'd lead to anything.'

He had finished his brandy and was looking at the bar-man in a particular way. If his train had had a restaurant car, he must have already had two or three drinks before arriving in Paris, because his face was red and his eyes glistened.

'Same again, inspector?'

Could it be that Maigret, too, had drunk more than he thought? He didn't say no. He felt fine, physically and mentally. He even had the impression that he was endowed with a sixth sense that allowed him to enter the skin of the people being talked about.

Would he have been capable of reconstructing the story

without Canonge's help? He hadn't been so far from the truth a few hours earlier, which was proved by the fact that he had thought of phoning Saint-André.

If he hadn't guessed everything, the idea he had got of Madame Calas nevertheless matched the one he might have of her now that he knew.

'She started drinking,' he murmured, with the sudden desire to talk in his turn.

'I know. I saw her.'

'When? Last week?'

On this point, too, he had sensed the truth. But Canonge wouldn't let him speak. In Saint-André he probably wasn't used to being interrupted.

'Let me take things in the order they happened, inspector. Don't forget I'm a lawyer, and lawyers are meticulous people.'

That made him laugh, and the girl sitting two stools away from him took advantage to ask him:

'Can I order a drink, too?'

'If you wish, my dear, provided you don't butt into our conversation. It's more important than you might think.'

Smugly, he turned to Maigret.

'Anyway, for three weeks my ad produced no results, apart from a few letters from crazy women. In the end, it wasn't the ad that led me to Aline, but pure chance. A week ago, a hunting rifle I'd sent to Paris to be repaired was returned to me, by express service. I was at home when it was delivered and so I was the one who opened the door to the lorry driver.'

'A lorry from Zenith Transport?'

'You know that? That's right. I offered the driver a glass of wine, as is the custom in the country. The Calas grocery is just opposite my house, on the church square. As he was having his drink, the man looked through the window and said:

'"I wonder if that's the same family that owns the bistro on Quai de Valmy."

'"Is there a Calas on the Quai de Valmy?" I asked.

'"A funny little bistro, where I'd never set foot before last week. It was one of the timekeepers who took me there."'

Maigret would have sworn that the timekeeper was none other than Dieudonné Pape.

'Did you ask him if the timekeeper had red hair?'

'No. I asked him the first name of this particular Calas. He started searching in his memory, vaguely remembering reading the name on the front of the bistro. I suggested Omer, and he said that was it. To be sure, I took a train to Paris the next day.'

'The evening train?'

'No. The morning one.'

'What time did you arrive at Quai de Valmy?'

'Just after three in the afternoon. In the bistro, which was quite dark, I saw a woman I didn't recognize immediately. I asked her if she was Madame Calas, and she said she was. Then I asked her her first name. She gave me the impression she was half drunk. She does drink, doesn't she?'

He, too, drank, not in the same way, but enough to now have watery eyes.

Maigret wasn't sure their glasses hadn't been filled

once again. The woman, who had changed stools, was leaning over Canonge and holding his arm. If she was following his story, nothing showed on her expressionless face.

'"You were born Aline de Boissancourt, weren't you?" I asked her.

'She looked at me and didn't deny it. I remember she was sitting near the stove with a big ginger cat in her lap.

'"Have you heard that your father has died?" I continued.

'She said she hadn't, but didn't show any surprise or emotion.

'"I was his lawyer, and now I'm handling his estate. Your father didn't leave a will, Madame Calas, which means that the chateau, the land and his entire fortune pass to you."

'"How did you get my address?" she asked.

'"I got it from a lorry driver who came here by chance."

'"Does anybody else know it?"

'"I don't think so."

'She stood up and went to the kitchen.'

To have a drink from the bottle of cognac, obviously!

'When she came back, she looked like someone who'd made up her mind.

'"I don't want that money," she declared in an indifferent voice. "I assume I have the right to give up the inheritance?"

'"Anyone has the right to refuse an inheritance. All the same . . ."

'"All the same what?"

'"I advise you to think it over and not come to a hasty decision."

'"I have thought it over. I refuse. I assume I also have the right to demand that you don't tell anyone where I am?"

'As she spoke, she occasionally threw an anxious glance outside, as if she was afraid of seeing someone walk in, maybe her husband. At least that's what I assumed.

'I insisted, as was my duty. I haven't found any other inheritors of Boissancourt.

'"It's probably best if I come back another time," I suggested.

'"No. Don't come back. Omer absolutely mustn't see you here. That would be the end of everything!" She seemed terrified.

'"Don't you think you should consult your husband?"

'"Especially not him!"

'I argued with her for a while longer, then got up to leave. I gave her my card and suggested she phone or write to me if she changed her mind over the next few weeks. A customer came in, who looked as if he was quite at home there.'

'A red-headed man with a pockmarked face?'

'I think so, yes.'

'What happened?'

'Nothing. She put my card in the pocket of her apron and walked me to the door.'

'What day was this?'

'Last Thursday.'

'Did you see her again?'

'No. But I saw her husband.'

'In Paris?'

'In my office, in Saint-André.'

'When?'

'Saturday morning. He arrived in Saint-André on Friday afternoon or Friday evening. The first time he came to see me was on Friday at about eight. I was at the doctor's house, playing bridge, and the maid told him to come back the next day.'

'Did you recognize him?'

'Yes, even though he'd put on weight. He must have been staying at the village inn, where, of course, he'd heard about Boissancourt's death. He must also have been told that his wife would inherit the family fortune. It didn't take him long to throw his weight around, claiming that as the husband he was entitled to accept the inheritance on behalf of his wife. They married without a contract, in other words under the convention of common assets.'

'Meaning one of them couldn't do anything without the other?'

'That's what I told him.'

'Did you have the impression that he'd had a conversation with his wife about this?'

'No. At first, he didn't even know she'd refused the inheritance. He seemed to think she'd got hold of it without his knowledge. I won't tell you the whole conversation, it would take too long. I think his wife must have left my card lying about, probably forgetting I'd given it to her, and he'd found it. What could have brought a lawyer from Saint-André to Quai de Valmy, unless it was something to do with the Boissancourt inheritance?

'It was only gradually, in my house, that he discovered the truth. He left in a rage, telling me that I'd be hearing from him and slamming the door.'

'Did you see him again?'

'No, and I didn't hear from him either. This happened on Saturday morning, and he took the bus to Montargis, where he caught the train for Paris.'

'Which train would that have been?'

'Probably the one that gets into the Gare d'Austerlitz just after three.'

That meant he had got home about four, a little earlier if he had taken a taxi.

'When I read that parts of a dismembered body had been found in the Canal Saint-Martin, on Quai de Valmy to be precise, I admit I was struck by the coincidence. As I told you earlier, I almost phoned you, then I told myself you might laugh at me. It was only when I heard the name Calas on the radio this afternoon that I made up my mind to come and see you.'

'May I?' the girl next to him asked, pointing to her empty glass.

'Yes, of course, my dear. What do you think of that, inspector?'

That word was enough for the girl to let go of his arm.

'I'm not surprised,' murmured Maigret, whose head was starting to feel heavy.

'Admit you never suspected a story like this! It's only in

the country that you encounter such bizarre characters, and even I confess . . .'

Maigret wasn't listening to him. He was thinking about Aline Calas, who had at last become a complete person in his mind. He could even imagine her as a little girl.

And this person didn't surprise him. He would have been hard put to explain it in words, especially to a man like Judge Coméliau, and he fully expected the latter's incredulous reaction the next day.

'The fact is,' Coméliau would reply, 'she committed a murder with the complicity of her lover.'

Omer Calas was dead, and he obviously hadn't killed himself. Someone must therefore have struck the fatal blow and then cut up his body.

Maigret thought he could hear Coméliau's shrill voice:

'I call that cold blood, don't you? You're surely not going to tell me it's a crime of passion? No, Maigret. I do sometimes agree with you, but this time . . .'

Canonge held up a full glass.

'Cheers!'

'Cheers!'

'What were you thinking about?'

'Aline Calas.'

'You think she followed Omer just to annoy her father?'

Even with Canonge, and even after a few glasses of brandy, it was impossible to express what he thought he understood. It was necessary first of all to admit that everything the girl had done at the Boissancourt chateau was already a protest.

Dr Pétrelle would no doubt have presented the case

better than he could. Her arson attempts, first of all. Then her sexual relations with Calas. Finally, her departure with Calas, while others in her situation would have provoked an abortion.

Perhaps it was also a kind of defiance? Or disgust?

Maigret had often tried to get other people, including men of experience, to admit that those who fall, especially those who have a morbid determination to descend ever lower and take pleasure in disgracing themselves, are almost always idealists.

It was pointless. Coméliau would reply:

'Let's just say she's always been depraved.'

On Quai de Valmy, she had started drinking. That fitted in with the rest. As did the fact that she had stayed, without ever being tempted to run away, and had clung to the atmosphere of the bistro.

He thought he understood Omer, too, Omer who had realized the dream of so many country boys: to earn enough money as a manservant or a chauffeur to become the owner of a bistro in Paris.

Omer led a lazy life there, dragging himself from the counter to the cellar, going once or twice a year to buy wine in the Poitou and spending his afternoons in a brasserie near Gare de l'Est playing belote or billiards.

They hadn't had time to investigate his private life. Maigret vowed to do so in the coming days, if only for his own satisfaction. He was convinced that, apart from his passion for billiards, Omer had brief, opportunistic affairs with young maids and female workers in the neighbourhood.

Had he been expecting the inheritance? It was unlikely: like everyone else, he must have thought that Boissancourt had disowned his daughter.

It had taken the lawyer's business card to give him hope.

'What I can't understand,' Canonge said, 'what's beyond me, my dear Maigret – and I've seen all kinds of heirs in my time – is that she could have refused a heaven-sent fortune.'

For Maigret, on the other hand, it was only natural. What would the money have brought her at this stage in her life? Would she have moved to the chateau with Omer? Would they have started leading, either in Paris or elsewhere, on the Riviera, for instance, a life modelled on that of the upper middle classes?

She had preferred to stay in her place, a place she had made for herself, rather like an animal in its burrow.

There, she would spend days that were all alike, with swigs of cognac behind the kitchen door and a visit from Dieudonné Pape in the afternoon.

He, too, had become a habit. More than that, perhaps, because he knew, and she wasn't ashamed in front of him, and they could sit together by the stove, in silence.

'Do you think she killed him?'

'I don't think so.'

'What about her lover?'

'That's quite likely.'

The musicians were putting away their instruments. Here, too, they were about to close. Maigret and Canonge found themselves back out on the street and set off in the direction of Saint-Germain-des-Prés.

'Do you live far?'

'Boulevard Richard-Lenoir.'

'I'll walk part of the way with you. Why did her lover kill Omer? Was he hoping to persuade her to accept the inheritance?'

They were both unsteady on their feet but they felt good, walking the streets of Paris, where the only thing to disturb them every now and again was a passing taxi.

'I don't think so.'

The next day, he would have to talk to Coméliau in another tone, because he realized there was something sentimental in his voice.

'Why did he kill him?'

'What do you think Omer's first concern was when he got back from Saint-André?'

'I don't know. I assume he was angry and ordered his wife to accept the money.'

An image came back to Maigret's memory: a bottle of ink and a blotting pad containing a few sheets of white paper, on the table in the bedroom.

'That's in his character, isn't it?'

'Very much so.'

'Let's suppose Omer tried to force her to sign a paper saying she accepted and she dug her heels in.'

'He was the kind of man who'd have given her a thrashing. I know our peasants.'

'He did occasionally beat her.'

'I'm starting to see what you're getting at.'

'When he comes back, he doesn't bother to change. It's

Saturday afternoon, about four. He gets Aline to come upstairs, orders her about, threatens her, hits her.'

'And then her lover arrives?'

'That's the most plausible explanation. Dieudonné Pape knows the house. Hearing the noise on the first floor, he crosses the kitchen and goes upstairs to rescue Aline.'

'And kills the husband!' Canonge concluded humorously.

'He kills him, deliberately or accidentally, by hitting him on the head with some instrument or other.'

'After which he cuts him up into pieces.'

That drew laughter from Canonge, who was in a jovial mood.

'Priceless! And what really strikes me as priceless is the idea of cutting Omer up into pieces. I mean, if you'd known Omer . . .'

Instead of sobering him up, the fresh air merely accentuated the effects of the alcohol.

'Will you walk back with me a little way?'

They both retraced their steps, then turned and did the same thing again.

'He's a curious man,' Maigret sighed.

'Who? Omer?'

'No, Pape.'

'To top it all, his name's Pape?'

'Not just Pape, but Dieudonné Pape.'

'Priceless!'

'He's the quietest man I've ever met.'

'Is that why he cut Omer up into pieces?'

It was true: it took a man like him, solitary, patient,

meticulous, to so successfully erase the traces of a murder. Even Moers and his men, with all their equipment, had found nothing in the house on Quai de Valmy to prove that a crime had been committed there.

Had Aline Calas helped to clean everything thoroughly and dispose of the linen and any objects that might have borne incriminating stains?

Pape had made only one mistake, a hard one to avoid, as it happened: he hadn't foreseen that Maigret would be surprised at the lack of dirty washing in the house and would think of asking the laundry.

What had the couple hoped? That weeks or months would pass before parts of Calas' remains would be found in the canal, and that by then these remains would be impossible to identify? That was what would have happened if the Naud brothers' barge hadn't been transporting a few tonnes of freestone too many and hadn't scraped the sludge at the bottom of the canal.

Had the head been thrown in the Seine or in a sewer? Maigret might know in a few days. He was convinced he would know everything in the end, yet that no longer aroused anything in him but a technical curiosity. What mattered was the drama that had played itself out among the three protagonists, and about that he was convinced he wasn't wrong.

He would have sworn that, once all trace of the crime had been erased, Aline and Pape had entertained the hope of a new life, not very different from the previous one.

For a time, Pape would have continued, as he had in the

past, to spend an hour or two every afternoon in the little bistro. Gradually, his visits would have grown longer until, with the husband forgotten by the customers and the neighbours, he moved in for good.

Would Aline have continued to let Antoine Cristin and others have their way with her?

It was possible. Maigret didn't dare venture into such deep waters.

'This time, I'll say goodnight!'

'May I phone you tomorrow at the hotel? I'll need you for a certain number of formalities.'

'You won't need to phone. I'll be at your office at nine o'clock.'

Of course, at nine o'clock, Canonge hadn't arrived, and Maigret had forgotten that he had promised to be there. He himself didn't feel too lively, and it was with a sense of guilt that he had opened his eyes when his wife, after putting his coffee down on the bedside table, had touched his shoulder.

She had an odd smile, more maternal than usual and quite tender.

'How do you feel?'

He couldn't remember ever having such a bad headache on waking, which meant that he had drunk a lot. He had seldom come home drunk, and what most annoyed him was that he hadn't been aware of drinking. It had happened gradually, one glass after another.

'Do you remember everything you told me last night about Aline Calas?'

He preferred not to remember, because he had the impression he had become more and more sentimental.

'You sounded as if you were in love with her. If I were a jealous woman . . .'

He blushed, and she hastened to reassure him.

'I'm joking. Are you going to tell all this to Coméliau?'

So he'd told her about Coméliau, too? That was indeed what remained for him to do. Only, he wouldn't talk to him in the same terms!

'Anything new, Lapointe?'

'Nothing, chief.'

'Can you put an ad in this afternoon's newspapers asking the young man someone asked to deposit a suitcase at Gare de l'Est on Sunday to make himself known to the police?'

'Wasn't it Antoine?'

'I'm convinced it wasn't. Pape wouldn't have asked someone who was a regular.'

'The man at the left luggage office says—'

'He saw a young man about the same age as Antoine, wearing a leather jacket. There are plenty of people around here who answer that description.'

'Do you have any evidence against Pape?'

'He'll confess.'

'Are you going to interrogate them?'

'I think at this point in the investigation, Coméliau will want to deal with that himself.'

It was becoming easy. It was no longer a question of asking questions haphazardly – fishing, as they called it at headquarters. Maigret wasn't even sure he was all that determined to force a confession out of Aline Calas and Dieudonné. They would both struggle to the end, until they could no longer keep silent.

He spent more than an hour upstairs in the magistrate's office. From there he called Maître Canonge, who must have woken with a start when the telephone rang.

'Who is it?' he asked, in such a strange way that Maigret smiled.

'Detective Chief Inspector Maigret.'

'What time is it?'

'Half past ten. Judge Coméliau, the examining magistrate in charge of the Calas case, would like to see you in his office as soon as possible.'

'Tell him I'll be right there. Shall I bring the Boissancourt papers?'

'If you like.'

'I hope you didn't get to bed too late because of me?'

Canonge must have gone to bed even later. God alone knew where he had wandered when Maigret had left him. At the end of the line, the inspector heard a woman's voice ask lazily:

'What time is it?'

Maigret went back down to his office.

'Is he going to interrogate them?' Lapointe asked.

'Yes.'

'Starting with the woman?'

'I advised him to start with Pape.'

'Will he come clean more easily?'

'Yes. Especially if, as I assume, he's the one who struck the fatal blow.'

'Are you going out?'

'I have something to find out at the Hôtel-Dieu.'

It was only a point of detail. He had to wait for the end of an operation in progress to see Lucette Calas.

'I suppose you've read in the newspapers about your father's death and your mother's arrest?'

'Something like that was bound to happen.'

'When you went to see her the last time, was it to ask her for money?'

'No.'

'Why, then?'

'To tell her I'm going to marry Professor Lavaud as soon as he gets his divorce. He may be curious to meet my parents, and I would have liked her to be presentable.'

'You didn't know that Boissancourt was dead?'

'Who's he?'

Her surprise was genuine.

'Your grandfather.'

He added in a neutral tone, as if announcing some unimportant news:

'Unless she's convicted of murder, your mother inherits a chateau, eighteen farms and I don't know how many millions.'

'Are you sure?'

'You can see Maître Canonge the lawyer, who's handling the estate. He's staying at the Hôtel d'Orsay.'

'Will he be there all day?'

'I assume so.'

She didn't ask him what would happen to her mother, and he left her, shrugging his shoulders.

Maigret didn't have lunch that day, because he wasn't hungry, but two glasses of beer more or less settled his stomach. He spent the whole afternoon shut up in his office. He had put the keys to the bistro and Pape's apartment down on the desk in front of him and he seemed to take a wicked pleasure in polishing off the bureaucratic chores he usually hated.

Whenever the telephone rang, he would pick it up more briskly than usual, but it wasn't until a few minutes after five o'clock that he recognized Coméliau's voice at the other end of the line.

'Maigret?'

'Yes.'

The judge could hardly contain a quiver of triumph.

'I was right to have them arrested.'

'All three of them?'

'No. I've just released young Antoine.'

'Have the others confessed?'

'Yes.'

'Everything?'

'Everything *we* assumed. I had the good idea of starting with the man. When I'd finished giving a detailed account of what must have happened, he didn't deny any of it.'

'What about the woman?'

'Pape repeated his confession in her presence. There was no way she could deny it.'

'Did she add anything?'

'As she left my office, she simply asked me if you'd taken care of her cat.'

'What did you tell her?'

'That you had other things to do.'

For the rest of his life, Maigret would resent Judge Coméliau for that remark.

OTHER TITLES IN THE SERIES

MAIGRET AT THE CORONER'S
GEORGES SIMENON

'The FBI man was convinced, in short, that Maigret was a big shot in his own country but that here, in the United States, he was incapable of figuring out anything . . . well, Maigret happened to believe that men and their passions are the same everywhere.'

Maigret is touring the United States to observe American policing methods when a visit to a coroner's inquest in Arizona draws him into the tragic story of a young woman and five airmen in the desert.

Translated by Linda Coverdale

INSPECTOR MAIGRET

OTHER TITLES IN THE SERIES

MAIGRET GETS ANGRY
GEORGES SIMENON

'All that was still unclear, for sure. Ernest Malik had been right when he had looked at Maigret with a smile that was a mixture of sarcasm and contempt. This wasn't a case for him. He was out of his depth. This world was unfamiliar to him, and he had difficulty piecing it together.'

Peacefully tending his garden in the countryside, Maigret is cajoled out of retirement by a case involving an old classmate and a rich family with skeletons in their cupboard – and finds himself confronted by lies, snobbery and malice.

Translated by Ros Schwartz

INSPECTOR MAIGRET

OTHER TITLES IN THE SERIES

MAIGRET IN NEW YORK
GEORGES SIMENON

'What was it about him that had struck Maigret so forcefully? . . .

Little John had cold eyes! . . .

Four or five times in his life, he had met people with cold eyes, those that can stare at you without establishing any human contact'

Persuaded to sail to New York by a fearful young law student, Maigret finds himself drawn into the city's underworld, and a wealthy businessman's closely guarded past.

Translated by Linda Coverdale

OTHER TITLES IN THE SERIES

MAIGRET TAKES A ROOM
GEORGES SIMENON

'What he thought he had discovered, in place of the joyful candour that she usually displayed, was an irony which was neither less cheerful nor less childish, but which troubled him . . .

He wondered now if his exultation wasn't down to the fact that she was playing a part, not just to deceive him, not just to hide something from him, but for the pleasure of acting a part.'

When one of his best inspectors is shot, Maigret decides to book himself into Mademoiselle Clément's well-kept Paris boarding house nearby in order to find the culprit.

Translated by Shaun Whiteside

INSPECTOR MAIGRET

OTHER TITLES IN THE SERIES